Mary Elizabeth Braddon

Darrell Markham: The captain of the Vulture

A novel

Mary Elizabeth Braddon

Darrell Markham: The captain of the Vulture
A novel

ISBN/EAN: 9783337197650

Printed in Europe, USA, Canada, Australia, Japan

Cover: Foto ©Andreas Hilbeck / pixelio.de

More available books at **www.hansebooks.com**

DARRELL MARKHAM;

OR THE

CAPTAIN OF THE VULTURE.

A NOVEL.

BY

M E BRADDON,

AUTHOR OF "LADY AUDLEY'S SECRET," "AURORA FLOYD," "JOHN MARCHMONT'S LEGACY,"
"THE LADY LISLE." ETC.

RICHMOND:
AYRES & WADE,
ILLUSTRATED NEWS STEAM PRESSES.
1863.

DARRELL MARKHAM;

OR THE

CAPTAIN OF THE VULTURE.

CHAPTER I.—THE WAY TO MARLEY WATERS.

'No one by the *Highflyer* to-night?' asked the blacksmith of Compton-on-the-Moor of the weak-eyed landlord of the Black Bear, first and greatest hostelry in that parish.

'No one but Captain Duke.'

'What? the Captain's been up in London, then, maybe?'

'Been there three weeks, and over,' replied the landlord, who seemed rather of a despondent nature, and not conversationally inclined.

'Ah! um!' said the blacksmith; 'three weeks and more up in London; three weeks and more away from that pretty-spoken lady of his; three weeks gambling, and roystering, and fighting, and beating of the watch, and dancing at that fine roundabout place at Chelsea, and suppers in Covent Garden; three weeks spending of the King's money; three weeks——'

'Going to the devil! three weeks going to the devil!' said a voice behind him; 'why not say it in plain English, John Homerton, while you're about it?'

'Bless us and save us, if it isn't Mr. Darrell Markham!'

'Himself, and nobody else,' said the speaker, a tall man in a riding-dress and high boots, wearing a three-cornered hat, drawn very much over his eyes; 'but keep it dark, Homerton, nobody in Compton knows I'm here; it's only a business visit, and a flying visit I'm off in a couple of hours. What was that you were saying about Captain George Duke, of his Majesty's ship the *Vulture?*'

'Why, I was saying, Master Darrell, that if I had such a pretty wife as Mistress Duke, and could only be with her two months out of the twelve, I wouldn't be in London half of the time. I think your cousin might have made a better match of it, Master Darrell Markham, with her pretty face.'

'I think she might, John Homerton.'

They had been standing at the door of the inn during this little dialogue. The blacksmith had the bridle of his sturdy little white pony—five-and-twenty years of age, if a day—in his hand, ready to mount him and ride home to his forge, at the furthest end of the straggling country town; but he had been unable to resist the fascination of the weak-eyed landlord's conversational powers. Darrell Markham turned away from the two, and walking out into the dusty high road, looked along a narrow winding track that crossed the bare black moorland, stretching away for miles before him. The Black Bear stood at the entrance to the town, and on the very edge of the bleak open country

'We shall have a dark night,' said Markham, 'and I shan't have a very pleasant ride to Marley Water'

'You'll never go to-night, sir!' said the landlord.

'I tell you I must go to-night, Samuel Pecker. Foul or fair weather, I must sleep at Marley Water this night.'

'You always was such a daring one, Mr. Darrell,' said the blacksmith, admiringly.

'It doesn't take so very much courage for a lonely ride over Compton Moor as all that comes to, John Homerton. I've a pair of pistols that never missed fire yet; my horse is sound, wind and limb; I've a full purse, and I know how to take care of it; I've met a highwayman before to-night, and I've been a match for one before to-night; and what's more to the purpose than all, Honest John, I *must* do it.'

'Must be at Marley Water to-night, Mr. Markham?'

'Must sleep at the Golden Lion, in the village of Marley Water, this night, Mr. Pecker,' replied the young man.

'Landlord, show me the road from here to Marley Water,' said a stranger.

The three men looked up, and saw, looking down at them, a man on horseback, who had ridden up to the inn so softly that they had never heard the sound of his horse's hoofs. How long the horse might have been standing there, or when the horseman had stopped, or where he had come from, neither of the three could guess; but there he was, with the last fading light of the autumn evening full upon his face, the last rosy shadow of the low sun gleaming on his auburn hair.

This face, lit up by the setting sun, was a very handsome one. Regular features, massively cut; a ruddy color in the cheeks, something bronzed by a foreign sun; brown eyes, with dark, clearly-defined eyebrows, and waving auburn hair, which the October breeze caught up from the low broad forehead. The horseman was of the average height, stalwart, well proportioned; a model, in short, of manly English beauty. The horse was like its master, broad-chested and strong-limbed.

'I want to know the nearest road to Marley Water,' he said for the second time; for there was something so sudden in the manner of his appearance, that neither of the three men had answered his inquiry.

The landlord, Mr. Samuel Pecker, was the first to recover from his surprise.

'Yon winding road across the moor will take you straight as an arrow, Captain,' he answered, civilly, but paradoxically.

The horseman nodded. 'Thank you, and good-night,' he said, and cantered along the moorland bridle-path, for the road was little better.

'Captain! who is he then?' asked Darrell Markham, as soon as the stranger was gone.

'Your cousin's husband, sir; Captain George Duke.'

'Is that George Duke? Why he spoke like a stranger.'

'That's his way, sir,' said the landlord; "that's the worst of the Captain; hail fellow well met, and what would you like to drink? one day, and keep your distance another. There's no knowing where to have him; but, after all, he's a jolly chap, the Captain.'

'He's a very handsome chap,' said Darrell Markham ; 'I don't so much wonder that Millicent Markham fell in love with him'

'There's some as says Miss Millicent had fell in love with some one else before she saw him,' said the landlord, insinuatingly.

'They should find something better to do than to talk of a young lady's love affairs, then,' answered Markham, gravely. 'I tell you what, Samuel Pecker, if I don't set out at once, I shan't find Marley Water to-night; it will be as dark as pitch in another hour. Tell them to bring out Balmerino.'

'Must you go to-night, Mr. Markham?'

'I tell you I must, Samuel. Come, tell the ostler to bring the horse round. I shall be half way there before 'tis dark, if I start at once.'

'Good-night, then, sir,' said the blacksmith ; 'I only wish you was going to stop in Compton ; the place is dull enough now, with the old squire dead, and the Hall shut up, and the young squire ruining himself at London, and you away. Compton isn't what it was when you was a boy, Mr. Darrell, and the the squire, your uncle, used to keep Christmas up at the Hall ; those were times—and now——'

'Egad, we must all get old, John Homerton,' said Darrell, with a sigh.

'But it's hard to sigh, or to talk of growing old either, sir,' said the blacksmith, 'at eight-and-twenty years of age. Good-night, Master Darrell, and—asking pardon for the liberty—God bless you,' and he mounted the elderly white pony, and jogged off towards the twinkling lights of the narrow high street.

Just as the blacksmith rode away, a female voice in the interior of the inn was heard crying, "Where is he?—where is that foolish boy of mine, I say? He's not a going away to-night ; he's not a going to have his throat cut, or his brains blowed out on the King's highway;' and with these words a ponderous female, of some fifty summers, emerged from the inn door, and flung two very red fat arms, ornamented with black mittens, round Darrell Markham's neck.

'You're not a going to-night, Master Darrell? Oh, I heard Pecker asking of you to stay ; but in *his* niminy piminy, namby pamby way, asking isn't asking, somehow,' said ponderous Mrs. Pecker, contemptuously. 'Oh, I've no patience with him ; as if you was a going to stay for dying ducks!' This rather obscure observation was pointed derisively at Mr. Samuel Pecker, whose despondent manner drew upon him the contempt of his magnificent and energetic better half.

As to the landlord of the Black Bear, it must be here set down that there was no such thing. Waiters there were, chambermaids there were, ostlers there were, but landlord there was not. He was so entirely absorbed in the splendor of his large and dominant spouse that he had much better not have been at all; for what there was of him was always in the way. If he gave an order, it was, of course, an insane and utterly impracticable order ; and if by any evil chance some domestic, unused, perhaps, to the ways of the place, attempted to execute that order, why there was the whole internal machinery of the Black Bear thrown into confusion for an entire day. If he received a traveller, he generally gave that traveller such a dismal impression of life in general, and Compton-on-the-Moor in particular, that nine times out of ten the dispirited wanderer would depart as soon as his horse had had a mouthful of corn and a drink of water out of the great trough under the oak tree before the door. There never were so many highway-men on any road as on the roads he spoke of ; there never were going to be such storms as when he discoursed of the weather; there never were such calamities coming down upon poor old England as when he talked politics, or such bad harvests about to paralyse the country as when he conversed on agriculture.

Some people said he was gloomy by nature, and that (like that well-beloved king across the channel, who used to tell Madame de Pompadour to stop in the middle of a funny story,) it was pain to him to smile. Others, on the contrary, affirmed that he had been a much livelier man before his marriage, and that the weight of his happiness was too much for him; that he was sinking under the bliss of being allied to so magnificent a creature as Mrs. Samuel Pecker, and that his unlooked-for good fortune in the matrimonial line had undermined his health and spirits. Be it as it might, there he was, mildly despondent, and utterly powerless to combat with the contumely daily heaped upon his head by his lovely but gigantic partner, Sarah Pecker.

The stranger, on first becoming a witness of the domestic felicity within the Black Bear, was apt to imagine that Mr. Samuel Pecker was in a manner an intruder there; landlord on sufferance, and nominal proprietor; or, as one might say, host consort, only reigning by the right of the actual sovereign, his wife. But it was no such thing; the august line of Pecker, time out of mind, had been regnant at the Black Bear. The late Samuel Pecker, father of Samuel, husband of Sarah, was a burly, stalwart fellow, six feet high, if an inch, and as unlike his mild and feeble son as it is possible for one Englishman to be unlike another Englishman. From this father Samuel had inherited all those premises, dwelling-house, out-buildings, gardens, farm-yard, stables, cowhouses, pig-sties, known as the Black Bear. But Samuel had not long enjoyed his dominions. Six months after ascending the throne, or rather installing himself in the great oaken arm-chair in the bar parlor of the Black Bear, he had taken to wife Sarah, housekeeper to Squire Ringwood Markham, of the Hall, and widow to Thomas Masterson, mariner.

Thus it is that Sarah Pecker's two fat mottled arms are at this present moment clasped round Darrell Markham's neck. She had known Darrell from his childhood, and firmly believed that not amongst all the beaux who frequent Ranelagh and the coffee-houses, not in either of the king's services, not in Leicester-fields or Kensington, not at the 'Cocoa Tree,' 'White's,' nor 'Bellamy's;' in the Mall, or in Change Alley; at the Bath, or at Tonbridge Wells; not, in short, in any quarter of civilized and fashionable England, is there to be met with so handsome, so distinguished, so clever, so elegant, so brave, generous, fascinating, noble and honest a scapegrace as Darrell Markham, gentleman at large, and, what is worse, in difficulties.

'You wont go to-night, Master Darrell,' she said. 'You wont let it be said that you went away from the Black Bear to be murdered on Compton Moore. Jenny's basting a capon for your supper at this very minute, and you shall have a bottle of your poor uncle's own wine, that Pecker bought at the Hall sale.'

'It's no use, Mrs. Pecker; I tell you I musn't stay. I know how well Jenny can roast a capon, and I know how comfortable you can make your guests, and there's nothing I should like better than to stop, but I musn't; I want to catch the coach that leaves Marley Water at five o'clock to-morrow morning for York. I had no right to come to Compton at all, but I couldn't resist riding across to shake hands with you, Mrs. Sarah, for the sake of the old times that are dead and gone, and to ask the news of Nat Halloway, the miller, and Lucas Jordan, the doctor, and Selgood, the lawyer, and a few more of my old companions, and——, and——'

'And of Miss Millicent? Eh, Master Darrell? For all London's such a wide city, and there's so many of these fine painted madams flaunting along the Mall, full sail, in their pannier-hoops and French furbelows, you haven't quite forgotten Miss Millicent, eh, Darrell Markham?'

She had nursed him on her ample knees when he was but a tiny, swaddled baby, and she sometimes called him Darrell Markham, *tout court*.

'There was something wrong in that, Master Darrell.' There was a gay wedding a year ago at Compton church, and very grand and very handsome everything was; and sure the bride looked very lovely, but one thing was wrong, and that was the bridegroom.'

'If you don't want me to be benighted, or to have these very indifferent brains of mine blown out by some valiant knight of the road upon Compton Moor, you'd better let me be off, Mrs. Pecker! Mistress Pecker! oh, the good old days, the dear old days! when I used to call you Mistress Sally Masterson, in the housekeeper's room at the Hall.' He turned away from her with a sigh, and began whistling a plaintive old English ditty, as he stood looking out over the wide expanse of gloomy moorland.

The ostler brought the horse round to the inn door—a stout brown hack, sixteen hands high, muscular and spirit-looking, with only one speck of white about him, a long slender streak down the side of his head.

The young man put his arm caressingly round the horse's neck, and drawing his head down looked at him as he would have looked at a friend, of whose truth, in all a truthless world, he at least was certain.

'Brave Balmerino, good Balmerino,' he said, 'you've to carry me four-and-twenty miles across a rough country to-night. You've to carry me on an errand, the end of which perhaps will be a bad one; you've to carry me away from a great many bitter memories and a great many cruel thoughts; but you'll do it, Balmerino, you'll do it, wont you, old boy?'

The horse nestled his head against the young man's shoulder, and snuffed at his coat sleeve.

'Brave boy; that means yes,' said Markham, as he sprang into the saddle. 'Good night, old friends; good-bye, old home: as Mr. Garrick says in Mr. Shakespeare's play, 'Richard's himself again!' Good-bye'

He waved his hand and rode slowly off towards the moorland bridle-path, but before he had crossed the wide high road, the usually phlegmatic Samuel Pecker intercepted him, by suddenly rising up, pale of countenance and dismal of mien, under his horse's head.

Darrell pulled up with an abrupt jerk that threw Balmerino on his haunches, or he must inevitably have ridden over the landlord of the Black Bear.

'Mr. Darrell Markham,' said the moody innkeeper, very slowly, 'don't you go to Marley Water this night! Don't go! Don't ask me why, sir, and don't, sir, ask me wherefore; for I don't know wherefore, and I can't tell why; but don't go! I've got one of those what-you-may-call-'ems. I mean one of those feelings about me that says, as plain as words, 'don't do it.''

'What, a presentiment, eh, Pecker?'

'That's the dictionary word for it, I believe, sir. Don't go!'

'Samuel Pecker, I must. If I go to my death, through going to Marley Water, so be it; I go.' He shook the bridle on the horse's neck, and the animal sped off at such a rate that by the time Mr. Samuel Pecker had recovered himself sufficiently to look up, all he could see of Darrell Markham was a cloud of white dust hurrying over the darkening moorland before the autumn wind.

Mrs. Pecker stood under the wide thatched porch of the Black Bear, watching the receding horseman.

Poor Master Darrell! Brave, generous, noble Master Darrell! I only wish, for pretty Miss Millicent's sake, that Captain George Duke was a little like him.'

'But suppose Captain George Duke wishes nothing of the kind? How then, Mistress Pecker?'

The person who thus answered Mrs. Pecker's soliloquy was a man of average height, dressed in a naval coat and three-cornered hat, who had come up to the inn doorway as quietly as the horseman had done half an hour before.

For once the gigantic bosom of the unflinching Sarah Pecker quailed before one of the sterner sex: she almost stammered, that great woman, as she said, 'I beg your pardon, Captain Duke, I was only a thinking!'

'You were only a thinking aloud, Mistress Pecker. So you'd like to see George Duke, of His Majesty's ship the *Vulture*, a good-for-nothing, idling, reckless ne'er-do-well, like Darrell Markham, would you?'

'I tell you what it is, Captain; you're Miss Millicent's husband, and if—if you was a puppy dog, and she was fond of you, there isn't a word I could bring myself to say against you, for the sake of that sweet young lady. But don't you speak one bad word of Master Darrell Markham, for that's one of the things that Sarah Pecker will never put up with, while she's got a tongue in her head, and sharp nails of her own at her fingers' ends.'

The Captain burst into a long, ringing laugh; a laugh that had a silver music peculiar to itself. There were people in the town of Compton-on-the-Moor, in the seaport of Marley Water, and on board His Majesty's frigate the *Vulture*, who said that there were times when that laugh had a cruel sound in its music, and was by no means good to hear. But what man in authority ever escaped the breath of slander, and why should Captain Duke be more exempt than his fellows?'

'I forgive you, Mrs. Pecker,' he said. 'I forgive you. I can afford to hear people speak well of Darrell Markham. Poor devil, I pity him!' With which friendly remark the Captain of the *Vulture* strode across the threshold of the inn, and on the door-step encountered Mr. Samuel Pecker, who had, after his solemn adjuration to Darrell Markham, re-entered the hostelry by a side door that led through the stable yard.

If Captain George Duke, of His Majesty's navy, had been a ghost, his appearance on the step of the inn door could scarcely have more astonished the mild Samuel Pecker. He started back, and stared at the naval officer with his weak blue eyes opened to their very widest extent.

'Then you didn't go, Captain?'

'Then I didn't go? Didn't go where?'

'Didn't go to Marley Water?'

'Go to Marley Water! No! Who said I was going?'

The small remnant of manly courage left in Mr. Samuel Pecker after his surprise, was quite knocked out of him by the energetic tone of the Captain, and he murmured mildly,—

'Who said so? Oh! no one particular; only, only yourself!'

The Captain laughed his own ringing laugh once more.

'*I* said so, *I* said so, Samuel? When?'

'Half an hour ago. When you asked me the way there.'

'When I asked you the way to Marley Water! Why I know the road as well as I know my own quarter-deck.'

'That's what struck me at the time, Captain, when you stopped your horse at this door and asked me the way. I must say I thought it was odd.'

'I stopped my horse! When?'

'Half an hour ago.'

'Samuel Pecker, I haven't been across a horse to-day. I'm not over-attached to the brutes at the best of times, but to-night I'm tired out with my journey from London, and I've just come straight from my wife's tea-table, where I've been drinking a dish of sloppy bohea and going to sleep over woman's talk.'

'And yet Parson Bendham says there's no such things as ghosts!'

'Samuel Pecker, you're drunk.'

'I haven't tasted a mug of beer this day, Captain. Ask Sarah.'

'That he hasn't, Captain,' responded his spouse to this appeal. 'I keep my eye upon him too sharp for that.'

'Then what's the fool wool-gathering about, Mistress Sally?' said the Captain, rather angrily.

'Lord have mercy upon us! I don't know,' replied Mrs. Pecker, scornfully; 'he's as full of fancies as the oldest woman in all Cumberland; he's always a seein' of ghosts, and hobgoblins, and windin'sheets, and all sorts of dismals,' added the landlady, contemptuously, 'and unsettlin' his mind for business and book-keepin' I haven't common patience with him, that I hain't.'

Mrs. Pecker was very fond of informing people of this fact of her small stock of common patience in the matter of Samuel, her husband; and as all her actions went to confirm her words, she was no doubt pretty generally believed.

'Oh! never mind, it's no consequence, and it's no business of mine,' said the landlord with abject meekness; 'there was three of us that seen him, that's all!'

'Three of you as seen whom?' asked the Captain.

'As see him,—— as see——' the landlord gave a peculiar dry gulp just here, as if the ghost of something was choking him, and he was trying to exorcise it by swallowing hard,—'three of us see—*it!*'

'It? What?'

'The Captain that stopped on horseback at this door half an hour ago, and asked me the way to Marley Water.'

Captain Duke looked very hard into the face of the speaker; looked thoughtfully, gravely, earnestly at him, with bright, searching brown eyes; and then again burst out laughing louder than before. So much was he amused by the landlord's astonished and awe-stricken face, that he laughed all the way across the low old hall, laughed as he opened the door of the oak room in which the genteeler visitors at the Bear were accustomed to sit, laughed as he threw himself back into the great wooden chair by the fire, and stretched his legs out upon the stone hearth, till the heels of his boots rested against the iron dogs, laughed as he called-in Samuel Pecker, and could hardly order his favorite beverage—rum punch—for laughing.

The room was empty, and it was to be observed that when the door had closed upon the landlord, Captain Duke, though he still laughed, something contracted the muscles of his face, while the pleasant light died slowly out of his handsome brown eyes, and gave place to a settled gloom.

When the punch was brought him, he drank three glasses one after another. But neither the great wood fire blazing on the wide hearth, nor the steaming liquid, seemed to warm him, for he shivered as he drank.

He shivered as he drank, and presently he drew his chair still closer to the fire, planted his feet upon the two iron dogs, and sat looking darkly into the red, spitting, hissing blaze.

'My incubus, my shadow, my curse!' he said.   Only six words, but they expressed the hatred of a lifetime.

By and bye a thought seemed suddenly to strike him; he sprang to his feet so rapidly that he overset the heavy, high-backed oaken chair, and strode out of the room.

On the other side of the hall was situated the common parlor of the inn—the room in which the tradesmen of the town met every evening, the oak-room being sacred to a superior class of travelers, and to such men as the doctor, the lawyer, and Captain Duke.   The common parlor was full this evening, and a loud noise of talking and laughter proceeded from the open door.

To this door the Captain went, and removing his hat from his clustering auburn curls, which were tied behind with a ribbon, he bowed to the merry little assembly.

They were on their feet in a moment; Captain George Duke, of His Majesty's ship the *Vulture*, was a great man at Compton-on-the-Moor; his marriage with the only child of the late squire identifying him with the place, to which he was otherwise a stranger.

'Sorry to disturb you, gentlemen,' he said, graciously; 'is Pecker here?'

Pecker was there, but so entirely crestfallen and subdued that, on hearing himself asked for, he emerged from the head of the table, like some melancholy male Aphrodite rising from the sea, and uttered not a word.

'Pecker, I want to know the exact time,' said the Captain.   'My watch is out of order, and Mistress Duke has been so much occupied with reading Mr. Richardson's romances and nursing her lap-dog, that all the clocks at the cottage are out of order too.   What is it by your infallible oaken clock on the stairs, Samuel?'

The landlord rubbed his two little podgy hands through his limp, sandy hair, and seeming to feel better after that slight refreshment, retired silently to execute the Captain's order.   A dozen stout silver turnip-shaped chronometers, and great leather-encased Tompion watches, were out in a moment.

'Half-past seven by me;' 'a quarter to eight;' 'twenty minutes, Captain!' He might have had the choice of half a dozen different times had he liked, but he only said, quietly—

'Thank you, gentlemen, very much; but I'll regulate my watch by Pecker's old clock, for I think it keeps truer time than the church, the market, or the jail.'

'The jail's pretty true to time at eight o'clock on a Monday morning sometimes, though, Captain, isn't it?' said a little shoemaker, the wit of the village.

'Not half true enough sometimes, Mr. Tompkins,' said the Captain, winding up his watch, with a grave smile playing round his well-shaped mouth.   'If every body was hung that deserves to be hung, Mr. Tomkins, there'd be more room in the world for honest people. Well, Samuel, what's the exact time?'

'Ten minutes to eight, Captain Duke, and such a night! I looked out of the staircase window, and the sky's so black that it seems as if it would fall down upon our heads, if it wasn't for the wind a-stopping of it.'

'Ten minutes to eight; that's all right,' said the Captain, putting his watch into his pocket. He turned to leave the room, but stopped at the door and said, 'Oh, by-the-bye, worthy Samuel, at what time did you see my ghost?' He laughed as he asked the question, and looked round at the company with a smile and a malicious wink in the direction of the subdued landlord.

'Compton church clock was striking seven as he rode away across the moor, Captain. But don't ask me anything, don't, please, talk to me, he said forlornly; 'it's no consequence, it's not any business of mine, it doesn't matter to anybody, but——' he paused and repeated the swallowing process, '*I saw it!*'

The customers at the Black Bear were not generally apt to pay very serious attention to any remark emanating from the worthy landlord, but these three last words did seem to rather impress them, and they stared with seared faces from Samuel Peeker to the Captain, and from the Captain back to Samuel Peeker.

'Our jolly landlord has been a little too free with his own old ale, gentlemen,' said George Duke. 'Good-night.'

He left the room, and, returning to the oak parlor, flung himself once more into his old moody attitude over the blazing logs; staring gloomily into the red chasms in the burning wood; craggy cliffs and deep abysses, down which ever and anon some dying ember fell like a suicide plunging from the summit of a cliff to the fathomless gulf below.

The great brown eyes of the Captain looked straight and steadily into the changing pictures of the fire. He was so entirely different a creature to that man whose gay voice and light laugh had just resounded in the common parlor of the inn, that it would have been difficult for any one having seen him in one place to recognize him in the other.

He was not long alone, for presently Nathaniel Halloway, the miller dropped in, and joined the Captain over his punch; and by-and-bye Attorney Selgood, and Mr. Jordan, the surgeon—Dr. Jordan, *par excellence*, throughout Compton— came in, arm in arm. The four men were very friendly, and they sat drinking, smoking, and talking politics till midnight, when Captain George Duke started from his seat and was for breaking up the party.

'Twelve o'clock from the tower of Compton church,' he said, as he rose from the table. 'Gentlemen, I've a pretty young wife waiting for me at home, and I've a mile to walk before I get home; I shall leave you to finish your punch and your conversation without me.'

Nathaniel Halloway sprang to his feet. 'Captain Duke, you're not going to leave us in this shabby fashion. You're not on your own quarter-deck, remember; and you're not going to have it all your own way. As for the pretty little Admiral in petticoats at home, you can soon make it straight with her. Stop and finish the punch, man!' and the worthy miller, on whom the evening's potations had had some little effect, caught hold of the Captain's gold-laced cuff and tried to prevent his leaving the room.

George Duke shook him lightly off, and opening the door that led into the hall, went out, followed by the miller and his boon companions, Dr. Jordan and Lawyer Selgood.

The house, which had been so quiet five minutes before, was now all bustle and confusion. First and foremost there was worthy Mistress Sarah Pecker alternately bewailing, lamenting, and scolding at the very extremest altitude of her voice. Then there was Samuel, her husband, pale, aghast, and useless, getting feebly into everybody's way, and rapidly sinking beneath the combined effects of inward stupefaction and universal contumely. Then there was the ostler and two rosy-faced, but frightened looking chambermaids clinging to each other and to the cook-maid and the waiter; and in the centre of the hall the one cause of all this alarm and emotion lay stretched in the arms of two men, a letter-carrier and a farm laborer. Yes, with Mrs. Sarah Pecker kneeling by his side, adjuring him to speak, to move, to open his heavy eye-lids; silent, motionless, and rigid, lay that Darrell Markham, who, five hours before, had started in full health and strength, for the little seaport of Marley Water.

'We kicked over him in the path,' said one of the men; 'me and Jim Bowlder here of Squire Morris's at the Grange; we come slap upon him in the dark, so dark that we couldn't see whether he was a man or a dead sheep; but we got him up in our arms and felt that he was stiff with cold and damp—he might be murdered or he might be frozen; there was some wet about his chest and his left arm, and I know by the feel of it, thick and slimy, that it was blood; and me and Jim Bowlder, we raised him between us, heels and head, and carried him straight here.'

'Who is it, what is it?' asked Captain Duke, advancing into the very heart of the little crowd.

'Your wife's nearest kinsman and dearest friend, Captain; Miss Millicent's first cousin, Darrell Markham! Murdered! murdered on the moorland road from here to Marley Water.'

'Not above a mile from here, missus,' interposed the laborer who had picked up the wounded man.

'Darrell Markham! my wife's cousin, Darrell Markham! What did he come here for? What was he doing in Compton?' The dark brown eyes looked straight down at the still face lying on the letter-carrier's shoulder, and dripping wet with the vinegar and water with which Mistress Pecker was bathing the sufferer's forehead.

'What did he come here for? He came here to be murdered! He came here to have his precious life taken from him upon Compton Moor, poor dear lamb, poor dear lamb!' sobbed Mrs. Pecker.

During all this confusion, Lucas Jordan, the surgeon, slid quietly behind the little crowd, and taking Darrell Markham's arm in his hand, deliberately slashed open his coat sleeve from the cuff to the shoulder with the scissors hanging at Mrs. Pecker's waist.

'A basin, Molly,' he said quietly. The terrified chambermaid brought him one in her shaking hands and held it under Darrell's arm.

'Steadily, my girl,' said the doctor, as he drew out the lancet and inserted it in the cold and rigid arm. The blood trickled slowly and fitfully from the vein.

'Is he dead, is he dead, Mr. Jordan,' cried Sarah Pecker.

'No more than I am, ma'am—no more than I am, Mrs. Pecker. A pistol bullet through the right arm, shivering the bone above the elbow. He has fainted from the loss of blood and the coldness of the night air. A few bruises and contusions from falling off his horse, and a wound in the scalp from the sharp pebbles on the road; nothing more.'

Nothing more! It seemed so little to these terrified people, who a minute before had thought him dead, that Mrs. Pecker, albeit unused to the melting mood, caught the surgeon's hand between her two fat palms and covered it with kisses and tears.

'So this is Darrell Markham,' said the Captain thoughtfully; 'Darrell, the irresistible; Darrell that was to have married his cousin Millicent, now my wife. Hum, a fair young man with auburn ringlets and a straight nose! No fear of his life, you say, doctor?'

'None, unless fever should supervene; which heaven forbid.'

'But if it should, how then?'

'Every fear. With the excitable temperaments——'

'His temperament is excitable?'

'Extremely excitable! An accident such as this is very likely to result in fever; fever may produce delirium. Mrs. Pecker, he must be kept very quiet, he must see no one—that is to say, no one whose presence can be in the least calculated to agitate him.'

'I'll keep watch at his door myself, doctor, and I should like to see,' said the worthy matron, glaring vengefully at her small spouse, 'I should very much like to see the person that'll dare to disturb him by so much as breathing.' The landlord of the Black Bear left off breathing on the instant, as if he imagined himself called upon to exist in future without the aid of that useful exercise.

'We must get him up stairs at once, Mrs. Pecker,' said the doctor. 'We must get him into your quietest room and your most comfortable bed, and we must lose no time about it.'

At the doctor's direction, the letter carrier and the farm laborer resumed their station at the head and feet of Darrell Markham, the ostler assisting them. The three men had just raised him in their arms, when he lifted his left hand to his damp forehead and slowly opened his eyes.

The three men stopped, and Mrs. Pecker screamed aloud, 'Oh, be joyful, he isn't dead! Master Darrell, speak to us, dear, and tell us you're not dead.'

The blue eyes looked dimly into the scared faces crowding round.

'He shot me. He robbed me of the letter to the king and of my purse. He shot me in my arm.'

'Who shot you, my darling? who shot you, Master Darrell, dear?' cried Mrs. Pecker.

The young man looked at her with a vacant stare, evidently half unconscious of where he was, and of the identity of those around him. Presently he took his blood-shot eyes from her face, and his gaze wandered round amongst the other spectators. From the landlord to the chambermaid, from the chambermaid to the letter-carrier, from the letter-carrier to the doctor, from the doctor to Captain George Duke, of his Majesty's ship the Vulture.

The blue eyes opened to their wildest distension with a wild stare.

'That, that's the man!'

'What man, Master Darrell?'

'The man who shot me.'

'I thought we should have him delirious,' said the doctor, under his breath.

Captain Duke's dark eyebrows fell loweringly over his brown eyes, and a black shade spread itself about his handsome face.

'You're dreaming, darling,' said Mrs. Pecker, soothingly. 'What man, dear, and where is he?'

Darrell Markham slowly lifted his unwounded arm and pointed with a white and slender hand full at the dark face of the Captain of the *Vulture*.

'There!' he said, half raising himself in the arms of the men supporting him, and with the effort he sank back once more unconscious.

'I thought so,'' muttered Captain Duke.

'So did I, Captain,'' responded the doctor. 'We shall have him in a high fever, and then he may go off like the snuff of a candle.'

'And he must be kept quiet?' asked the Captain, as they carried the wounded man up the wide oak staircase.

'He must be kept quiet, Captain, or I'll not answer for his life. I've known him from a boy, and I know any strong excitement will throw him into a brain fever.'

'Poor fellow! He's a kinsman of mine, by my marriage with his cousin; though I'm afraid there's not much love lost between us on that score. And this is the first time we've met. Strange!'

'There's a good deal in life that is strange, Captain Duke,' said the doctor, sententiously.

'There is, doctor,' answered the sailor. 'So Darrell Markham, travelling from Compton to Marley Water, has been shot by a person or persons unknown. Very strange.'

CHAPTER II.—MILLICENT.

Millicent Duke sat alone in her little parlor on this autumn night, with the high wind howling and whistling round her windows, trying to read Mr. Richardson's last novel; a well thumbed little volume, embellished with small oval engravings, which had been lent to her by the wife of the curate of Compton-on-the-Moor. But she couldn't read; the book dropped out of her hands, and she fell a musing over the low fire and listening to the wind disporting itself in the chimney. It is something to be able to look at Mrs. Millicent Duke, as she sits quietly by her lonely hearth, with one white hand supporting her small head, and with her elbow leaning on the stiff horse-hair-cushioned arm of the chair in which she is seated.

It is a very fair and girlish face upon which the fitful firelight trembles; now illumining one cheek with a soft red glow, now leaving it in shadow as the flame shoots up or dies out of the scattered embers on the hearth. A very fair and girlish face, with delicate features and softly dark-blue eyes, that leave a sad shadow in their softness—a shadow as of tears long dried but not forgotten. There are pensive lines, too, about the mouth which do not tell of an entirely happy youth; sorrow and Millicent Duke have met each other face to face, and have been companions and bedfellows before to-night. But in spite of this pensive sadness which shadows her beauty, or perhaps by every virtue of this sadness, which refines the beauty it shadows, Millicent Duke is a very pretty girl. It is difficult to think of her as a married woman; there is such an air of extreme youth about her, such a girlish, almost childish timidity in her manner, that, as her husband—not too loving or tender a husband at the best of times—is apt to say, 'it is as difficult to deal with Millicent as with a baby, for you never know when she may begin whimpering like a spoiled child as she is.' There are people in Compton-on-the-Moor who remember the time when the spoiled child never whimpered, and when a gleam of spring sunshine was scarcely a brighter or more welcome thing to fall across a man's pathway than the radiant face of Millicent Markham; but this was in the good days long departed, when her father, the squire, was living, and when she used to ride about the country roads on her pretty white pony, accompanied and protected by her cousin and dearest friend, Darrell Markham.

She is peculiarly sad this night. The shrill wind whistling at the latticed casements makes her shiver to the heart; she draws the skirt of her grey silk petticoat over her shoulders, and drags the heavy chair nearer to the low fire; she has sent her one servant, a strapping country girl, to bed long ago, and she cannot get any more fuel to heap upon the wide hearth. The wax candles have burnt low in the quaint old silver candle-sticks; ten, eleven, twelve have struck, with long dreary intervals between each time of striking, from the tower of Compton church, and still no Captain Duke.

'He is happier with them than with me,' she said, mournfully. 'Who can wonder? They make him smile; I can only weary and annoy him with my wretched pale face.' She looked up as she spoke at an oval mirror on the wainscot opposite to her, and saw this sad pale face reflected by the faint light of the low fire and the expiring candles. 'And they once called me a pretty girl! I think he would scarcely know me now!' she said, with a sigh.

The long hour after midnight dragged itself out, and as one o'clock struck with a dismal sound vibrating drearily along the empty street, she heard the sharp stroke of her husband's footstep on the pavement. She sprang from her chair hurriedly, and ran out into the narrow passage; but just as she was about to withdraw the bolts, she paused suddenly, and laid her hand upon her heart. 'What -is the matter with me to-night—what is the matter, I wonder?' she murmured; 'I feel as if some great unhappiness were coming, yet what more unhappiness can come to me?'

Her husband knocked impatiently at the door with his sword-hilt, as she fumbled nervously with the bolts.

'Were you listening at the door, Millicent, that you open it so quickly?' he asked, as he entered.

'I heard your footstep in the street, George, and hurried to let you in. You are very late,' she added, as he strode into the parlor, and flung himself into the chair she had been sitting in.

'Oh, a complaint, of course,' he said, with a sneer. 'I've a great deal to keep me at home, certainly,' he muttered, looking round—'a crying wife and a bad fire.' He turned his back to her, and bent over the embers, trying to warm his hands at the red light left in them. She seated herself at the slender-legged polished mahogany table, and taking up Mr. Richardson's neglected novel, pretended to read it by the last glimmer of the two candles.

Presently he said, without once turning round to look at her, without once changing his stooping posture over the fireplace, without once addressing her by name; 'There's been an accident down there !'

'An accident!' She dropped her book, and looked up with an expression of vague alarm. 'An accident! Oh, I am sorry; but what accident?'

Though there was an accent of gentle pity in her voice, there was still a slight bewilderment in her manner, as if she were so preoccupied by some sad thoughts of her own as scarcely to be able to understand his words.

As he did not answer her first question, she asked again, 'What accident, George?'

'A man half killed by highwaymen on Compton Moor.'

'But not killed, George—not killed?' she asked, anxiously, but still with that half-preoccupied manner, as if, in spite of herself, she could not quite concentrate her mind upon the subject of which her husband was speaking.

'Not killed, no; but all but killed, don't I tell you?' said the Captain. 'Just the toss-up of a guinea whether he lives or dies. And a handsome fair-haired lad enough,' he added, half to himself—'a handsome, fair-faced, fair-haired lad enough. Poor devil!'

'I am very sorry,' she said, gently; and as her husband did not stir from his seat by the fire, she took up her book once more, and began poring over the small, old-fashioned type. Her husband turned and looked at her as she sat bending over the light, and after watching her for a few minutes with an angry glimmer in his handsome brown eyes, said, with a scornful laugh:

'Heaven bless these novel-reading women! The death of a fellow-creature is little enough to them as long as Miss Clarissa is reconciled with her lover, and Mistress Pamela's virtue is rewarded in the sixth volume! Here's a tender, compassionate creature for you! cries over Sir Charles Grandison, and doesn't so much as ask me who it is that is lying between death and life in the blue room down at the Black Bear!'

She looked up at him with a frightened face, as if she were used to hard words, and used to warding them off by apologetic speeches, and said hesitatingly :

'I beg your pardon, George! Indeed I am not unfeeling. I am sorry for this poor wounded, half-dying man, whoever he may be. If I could do anything to serve him, or to comfort him, I would do it. I would do it at whatever cost to myself. What more can I say, George?'

'And they talk about a woman's curiosity!' he cried, with a mocking laugh; 'even now she doesn't ask me who the wounded man is.'

'I do, I do, George. Poor creature! who is he?'

He paused for a few moments after her question. She had risen from her seat, and stood at the table trying to revive the drooping wick of the last of the two candles left burning. The Captain turned his chair full round, and watched her pale face as he said, slowly and distinctly—

'Your first cousin, Darrell Markham!'

She uttered a cry; not a shrill scream, but a faint, pitiful cry; and lifted her two little hands wildly to her head. She remained in this attitude for some minutes, quite still, quite silent, and then sank quietly into her old position at the table. Her husband watched her all the time with a sneering smile and bright glitter in his eyes.

'Darrell! my cousin Darrell dead?'

'Not dead, Mistress Millicent; not quite so bad as that. Your dear, fair haired, pretty-faced cousin is not dead, my sweet, loving wife; he is only—dying.'

'Lying in the blue room at the Black Bear,' she repeated the words he had said a few minutes before, in a distracted manner, very painful to look upon.

'Lying in the blue room at the Bear. Yes, the blue room, number four, on the long corridor. You know the chamber well enough; have you not been there often to see your father's old house-keeper, the mariner's widow, at least the inn-keeper's wife?'

'Trembling between life and death?' she said, in the same half-conscious, pitiful tone.

'He was! Heaven knows how he may be now. That was half an hour ago; the scale may be turned by this time; he may be dead!'

As he said the last word, she sprang from her seat, and, without once looking at him, ran hurriedly to the outer door. She had her hand upon the bolts, when she cried out in a tone of dismal anguish, 'Oh! no, no, no!' and dropped down on her knees, with her head leaning against the lock of the door.

The Captain of the *Vulture* followed her every movement with his eyes, and as she fell on her knees, he said—

'You were going to run to him!'

'I was.'

'Then, why not go? You see I am not cruel; I do not stop you. You are free! Go! Shall I open the door for you?'

She lifted herself with an effort upon her feet, still leaning for support against the street door. 'No,' she said, 'I will not go to him; I could do him no good; I might agitate him; I might kill him!'

The Captain bit his under lip, and the smile faded in his brown eyes.

'But understand this, George Duke; it is no fear of you which keeps me here; it is no dread of your cruel words or more cruel looks that holds me from going to his side; for if I could save him by my presence from one throb of pain, if I could give him by my love and devotion one moment's peace and comfort, and the town of Compton were one sea of raging fire, I would walk through that sea to do it.'

'That's a very pretty speech out of a novel,' said her husband, 'but I never very much believe in these pretty speeches—perhaps I've a good reason of my own for doubting them. I suppose if Darrell Markham asked for you with his dying breath you'd go to see him; especially,' he added, with his old sneer, 'as Compton *isn't* a sea of fire.' He rose as he said this, and came out into the passage, where she stood. She sprang towards him, and caught his arm convulsively between her two little hands. 'Did he, did he, did he?' she cried, passionately; 'did Darrell ask to see me? Oh, George Duke, on your honor as a gentleman, as a sailor, as a trusted servant of his gracious Majesty, by your hope in Heaven, by your faith in God, did Darrell Markham ask to see me?'

He kept her waiting for his answer as he slowly lit a wax taper at the flickering flame in the high candlestick.

'I shan't say no, and I shan't say yes,' he said; 'I'm not going to be go-between for you and him. Good night,' he added, passing her in the passage, and going slowly up the stairs; 'if you've a mind to sit up all night, do so, by all means. It's on the stroke of two, and I'm tired. Good night!'

2

He strode up stairs, and entered a little sleeping room over the parlor in which they had been seated. It was simply but handsomely furnished, and the most exquisite neatness prevailed in all its arrangements. A tiny fire burned on the hearth, but though the Captain shivered, it was to the window he directed his steps. He opened it very softly, and leaned out, as the clocks struck two. 'I thought so,' he said, as he heard the faint rattle of the bolts and the creaking of a door. 'By the heaven above me, I knew she would go to him!'

The faint echoes of a light and rapid footstep broke the silence of the quiet street. 'And the least agitation might be fatal!' said the Captain of the *Vulture*, as he softly closed the casement window.

Darrell Markham lay in a death-like stupor in the blue chamber at the Black Bear. Mr. Jordan, the doctor, had declared that his shattered arm, if it ever was set at all, could not be set for some days to come. In the meantime Mrs. Sarah Pecker had received directions to bathe it constantly with a cooling lotion, but on no account, should the young man again return to consciousness, was the worthy landlady of the Black Bear to disturb him with either lamentations or inquiries; neither was she, at hazard of his life, to admit any one into the room but the doctor himself. Mrs. Pecker devoted herself to her duties as nurse to the wounded man with a good will, merely remarking that she should very much like to see the individual, male or female, as would come anigh him, to worrit or to vex him; 'for if it was the parson of the parish,' she said, with determination, 'he musn't set much account on his eyesight if he tries to circumvent Sarah Pecker.'

'No one must come anigh him, once for all, and once and forever,' added Mrs. Pecker, sharply, as she faced about on the great staircase, and confronted a little crowd of pale faces, for all the household thronged round her when she emerged from the sick room in their eagerness to get tidings of Darrell Markham; 'and I won't have *you*,' she continued, with especial acerbity, to her lord and master, the worthy Samuel, 'I won't have *you* a comin' and a worritin' with your "Aint he better, Sarah?" and "Don't you think he'll get over it, Sarah?" and such like! When a poor dear young gentleman's arm is shivered to a jelly,' she said, addressing herself generally, 'and when a poor dear young gentleman has been a lying left for dead on a lonely moor for ever so many cruel hours on a cold October night, he don't get over it in twenty minutes, no, nor yet in half an hour neither! So what you've all got to do is just to go back to the kitchen, and sit there quiet till one or other of you is wanted, for whatever Muster Darrell wants shall be got! Yes, if he wanted the king's golden crown and sceptre one of you should walk to London and fetch 'em!' Having thus declared her supreme pleasure, Mrs. Pecker re-ascended the stairs, and re-entered the sick room.

'If a person could be in two places at once, any way convenient,' muttered the landlord, as he withdrew into the offices of the inn, 'why I could account for it most easy; but seein' they can't, or seein' as how the parson says they can't, it's too much for me,' upon which Mr. Samuel Pecker seated himself on a great settle before the kitchen fire, and began to scratch his head feebly.

'I think as Mr. Markham's had himself shot in the arm, and she aint over likely to be a comin' downstairs, I might venture on a mug of the eightpenny,' the landlord by-and-bye remarked, thoughtfully.

Half-past two by the eight-day clock on the stairs, and the landlord going to fetch himself this very mug of beer, was arrested in the hall by a feeble knocking at the stout oaken door, closed and barred for the night; for the doctor had determined on remaining with his patient till the following morning.

The candle nearly dropped from the hand of the nervous landlord. 'Ghosts, I dare say,' he muttered; 'Compton's full of 'em.' The knocking was repeated; this time a little louder.

'They knocks hard for spirits,' said Samuel, 'and they're pretty persevering' The knocking was still continued, still growing louder. 'Oh, then, I suppose I must,' murmured Mr. Pecker, with a groan; 'but when I undoes the bolts what's the good? Of course there's no one there.'

There was some one there, however, for when Mr. Pecker had undone the bolts very slowly, and very cautiously, and with a great many half-suppressed but captious groans, a woman slid in at the narrow opening of the door, and before Mr. Pecker had recovered his surprise, crossed the hall, and made direct for the forbidden room in which Darrell Markham lay.

Terror of the vengeance of the ponderous Sarah seized upon the soul of the landlord, and with an unwonted activity he ran forward, and intercepted the woman at the bottom of the stairs.

'You musn't ma'am,' he said, " you musn't; excuse me, ma'am, but its as much as my life, or even the parson—yes, ma'am, Sarah!' thus vaguely the terrified Samuel.

The woman let the large grey hood which muffled her face' fall back and said, 'Don't you know me, Mr. Pecker? 'Tis I, Millicent, Millicent—Duke.'

'You, Miss Millicent. You, Mrs. Duke. Oh, miss, oh, ma'am, your poor dear cousin!'

'Mr. Pecker, for the love of mercy, don't keep me from him. Stand out of the way, stand out of the way,' she said, passionately; ' he may die while your'e talking to me here.'

'But, ma'am, you musn't go to him; the doctor, ma'am, and Sarah, Miss Millicent. Sarah, she was quite awful about it, ma'am.'

' Stand aside,' she said; 'I tell you a raging fire shouldn't stop me. Stand aside!'

'No, ma'am—but Sarah!'

Millicent Duke stretched out two slender white hands, and pushed the landlord from her way with a strength that sent him sliding round the polished oak banister of the lowest stair. She flew up the flight of steps, which brought her to the door of the blue room, and on the threshold found herself face to face with Mrs. Sarah Pecker.

The girl fell on her knees, her pale hair falling loose about her shoulders, and her long grey cloak trailing round her on the polished oaken floor.

'Sarah, Sarah, darling Sarah, dear, let me see him.'

'Not you, not you, nor any one,' said the landlady, sternly—' you the last of all persons, Mrs. George Duke.'

The name struck her like a blow, and she shivered under the cruelty of the thrust.

'Let me see him!—let me see him!' she said; 'his father's brother's only child—his first cousin—his playfellow—his friend—his dear and loving friend—his——'

'Wife that was to have been, Mrs. Duke,' interrupted the landlady.

'His wife that was to have been; and never, never should have been another's. His loving, true, and happy wife, that would have been. Let me see him!' she cried piteously, holding up her clasped hands to Mrs. Pecker.

'The doctor's in there, do you want him to hear you, Mrs. Duke?'

'If all the world heard me I wouldn't stop from asking you: Sarah let me see my cousin, Darrell Markham!

The landlady, holding a candle in her hand, and looking down at the piteous face and tearful eyes all blinded by the loose, pale golden hair—softened a little as she said—

'Miss Millicent, the doctor has forbidden a mortal creature to come anigh him! the doctor has forbidden a mortal soul to say one word to him that could disturb or agitate him! and do you think the sight of your face wouldn't agitate him?'

'But he asked to see me, Sarah; he spoke of me!'

'When, Miss Millicent?' Softening towards this pitiful pale face looking up into hers, the landlady leaves off calling her dead master's daughter by this new name of Mrs. Duke. 'When, Miss Millicent?'

'To-night—to-night, Sarah.'

'Master Darrell asked to see you! Who told you that?'

'Captain Duke.'

'Master Darrell hasn't said better than a dozen words this night, Miss Millicent; and those words were mad words, and never once spoke your name.'

'But my husband said——'

'The Captain sent you here, then?'

'No, no; he didn't send me here. He told me—at least he gave me to understand that Darrell had spoken of me—had asked to see me.'

'Your husband is a strange gentleman, Miss Millicent.'

'Let me see him, Sarah, only let me see him. I won't speak one word, or breathe one sigh; only let me see him.'

Mrs. Pecker withdrew for a few moments into the blue room, and whispered to the doctor. Millicent Duke, still on her knees on the threshold of the half-opened door, strained her eyes as if she would have pierced through the thick oak that separated her from the wounded man.

The landlady returned to the door. "If you want to look at a corpse, Miss Millicent, you may come in and look at him, for he lies as still as one."

She took the kneeling girl in her stout arms, and half lifted her into the room, where, opposite a blazing fire, Darrell Markham lay unconscious on a great draperied four-post bed. His head was thrown back upon the pillow, the fair hair dabbled with a lotion with which Mrs. Pecker had been bathing the scalp-wound spoken of by the doctor. Millicent tottered to the bedside, and seating herself in an arm-chair which had been occupied by Sarah Pecker, took Darrell Markham's hand in her's, and pressed it to her tremulous lips. It seemed as if there was something magical in this gentle pressure, for the young man's eyes opened for the first time since the scene in the hall, and he looked at his cousin.

'Millicent,' he said, without any sign of surprise, 'dear Millicent, it is so good of you to watch me.' She had nursed him three years before through a dangerous illness, and in his delirium he confused the present with the past, fancying that he was in his old room at Compton Hall, and that his cousin had been watching by his bedside.

'Call my uncle,' he said, 'call the squire; I want to see him!' and then, after a pause, he muttered, looking about him, 'surely this is not the old room—surely some one has altered the room.'

'Master Darrell, dear,' cried the landlady, 'don't you know where you are? With friends, Master Darrell, true and faithful friends. Don't you know, dear?'

'Yes, yes,' he said, 'I know, I know, I've been lying out in the cold and my arm is hurt. I remember, Sally, I remember; but my head feels strange, and I can scarce tell where I am.'

'See here, Master Darrell, here's Mistress Duke has come all the way from the other end of Compton, on this bitter, black night, on purpose to see you.' The good woman said this to comfort the patient, but the utterance of that one name, Duke, recalled his cousin's marriage, and the young man exclaimed, bitterly,

'Mistress Duke! yes, I remember;' and then turning his weary head upon the pillow, he cried, with a sudden energy, 'Millicent Duke, Millicent Duke, why do you come here to torture me with the sight of you?'

At this moment there arose the sound of some altercation in the hall below, and then the noise of two voices in dispute and hurried footsteps upon the staircase. Mrs. Pecker ran to the door, but before she could reach it, it was burst violently open, and the Captain of the *Vulture* strode into the room. He was closely followed by the doctor, who walked straight to the bedside, exclaiming with suppressed passion, 'I protest against this, Captain Duke; and if any ill consequence come of it, I hold you answerable for the mischief.'

The Captain took no notice of this speech, but turning to his wife, said savagely, 'Will it please you to go home with me, Mistress Millicent?' It is near upon four o'clock, and a sick gentleman's room is scarce a fit place for a lady at such a time.'

Darrell Markham lifted himself up in the bed, and cried with a hysterical laugh, 'I tell you that's the man, Millicent; Sarah, look at him. That is the man who stopped me upon Compton Moor, shot me in the arm and rifled me of my purse.'

'Darrell! Darrell!' cried Millicent, 'you do not know what you are saying. That man is my husband.'

'Your husband! A highwayman!—a——'

Whatever word was on his lips remained unspoken, for he fell back insensible upon the pillow.

'Captain George Duke,' said the surgeon, laying his hand upon the patient's wrist, 'if this man dies, you have committed a murder.'

CHAPTER III.—LOOKING BACK.

John Homerton, the blacksmith, only spoke advisedly when he said that the young squire, Ringwood Markham, was ruining himself up in London.

Ringwood Markham was three years older than his sister Millicent, and six years younger than his cousin Darrell; for old Squire Markham had married late in life, and had, shortly after his marriage, adopted little Darrell, the only child of a younger brother, who had died early, leaving a small fortune to his orphan boy

Ringwood Markham in person, closely resembled his sister. He had the same pale, golden hair, the deep, limpid, blue eyes, the small features, and delicate pink and white complexion.

Ringwood had always been his father's favorite, to the exclusion even of pretty, loveable Millicent; and as his cousin Darrell grew to manhood, it vexed the old squire to see the elder, high-spirited and stalwart, broad-chested and athletic, accomplished in all manly occupations; a good shot, an expert swordsman, a bold horseman, and a reckless, dare-devil, generous, thoughtless, open-hearted lad, while Ringwood only thought of his pretty face and his embroidered waistcoat, and loved the glittering steel ornaments of his sword-hilt far better than the blade of that weapon.

It was hard for the squire to have to confess it, even to himself; but it was not the less a fact, that Ringwood Markham was a milksop.

The old man hated Darrell for being superior to his son.

This was how the pale face of sorrow first peeped in upon the little family group at Compton Hall.

Darrell and Millicent had loved each other from that early childish, but unforgotten day, on which the orphan boy peeped into his baby cousin's cradle, and cried out at her pretty face and tiny rosy hands.

They loved each other from such an early age, and they loved each other so honestly and truly, that perhaps they were never, in the legitimate sense of the word, lovers.

If the squire saw this growing attachment between the young people, he neither favored nor discouraged it. He had never cared much for Millicent. She and her brother were the children of a woman whom he had married for the sake of a handsome fortune, and who died unnoticed and unregretted, and, some people said, of a broken heart, before Millicent was a twelvemonth old.

So things went on pretty smoothly. Millicent and Darrell rode together through the shady green lanes, and over the stunted grass and heather on Compton Moor, while Ringwood idled about the village, or lounged at the bar of the Black Bear, until a catastrophe occurred which changed the whole current of events.

Darrell and Ringwood Markham had a desperate quarrel—a quarrel in which blows were struck and hard words spoken upon both sides, and which abruptly ended Darrell's residence at Compton Hall.

Darrell had discovered a flirtation between Ringwood and a girl of seventeen, the daughter of a small farmer—a flirtation which, but for this timely discovery, might have ended in shame and despair. Scarlet with passion, the young man had taken his foppish cousin by the collar of his velvet coat, and dragged him straight into the presence of the father of the girl, saying, with an oath, such as was, unhappily, only too common a hundred years ago—

'You'd better keep an eye on this young man, Farmer Morrison, if you want to save your daughter from a scoundrel.'

Ringwood turned very white—he was one of those who grew pale and not red with passion—and sprang at his cousin like a cat, caught at his throat as if he would have strangled him; but one swinging blow from Darrell's fist laid the young man on Farmer Morrison's sanded floor, with a general illumination glittering before his dazzled eyes.

Darrell strode back to the Hall, where he packed some clothes in his saddle-bags, and wróte two letters, one to his uncle; telling him, abruptly enough, that he had knocked Ringwood down because he had found him acting like a rascal, and that he felt, as there was now bad blood between them, they had better part. His second letter was addressed to Millicent, and was almost as brief as the first. He simply told her of the quarrel, adding that he was going to London to seek his fortune, and that he should return to claim her as his wife.

He left the letters on the high chimney-piece in his bedroom, and went down to the stables, where he found his own nag Balmerino, and fastened his few possessions to the saddle, mounted the horse in the yard, and rode slowly away from the house in which his boyhood and youth had been spent.

Ringwood Markham went home late at night with a pale face and a handker-chief bound about his forehead.

He found his father sitting over a spark of fire in the oak parlor on one side of the hall. The door of this parlor was ajar, and as the young man tried to creep past, on his way up stairs, the squire called to him sharply, ' Ringwood, come here.'

He cowered sulkily into the room, hanging his broken head down, and looking at the floor.

' What's the matter with your head, Ringwood ?'

' The pony shied at some sheep on the moor, and threw me against a stone,' muttered the young man.

' You're telling a lie, Ringwood Markham. I've a letter from your cousin Darrell in my pocket. Bah, man! you're the first of the Markhams that ever took a blow without paying it back with interest. You've your mother's milk-and-water disposition, as well as your mother's face.'

' You needn't talk about her,' said Ringwood ; ' you didn't treat her too well, if folks speak the truth.'

' Ringwood Markham, don't provoke me. It's grief enough to have a son that can't take his own part. Go to bed.'

The young man left the room with the same slouching step with which he had entered. He stole cautiously up stairs, for he thought his cousin Darrell was still in the house, and he had no wish to arouse that gentleman.

So Millicent was left alone at Compton Hall. Utterly alone, for she had now no one to love her.

Darrell, therefore, being gone, and dear old Sally Masterson having left the Hall to be mistress of the Black Bear, poor Millicent was abandoned to the ten-der mercies of her father and brother, neither of whom cared much more for her than they did for the meek white and liver-coloured spaniel that followed her about the house. So the delicate piece of mechanism got out of order, and Mil-licent's days were devoted to novel reading and to poring over an embroidered waistcoat-piece that was destined for Darrell, and the colors of which were dull and faded from the tears that had dropped upon the silks.

She kept Darrell's letter in her bosom. In all the ways of the world she was as unlearned as in that day when Darrell had peeped in upon her asleep in the cradle, and she had no more doubt that her cousin would make a fortune, and re-turn in a few years to claim her as his wife, than she had of her own existence. But, in spite of this hope, the days were long and dreary, her father neglectful, her brother supercilious and disagreeable, and her home altogether very miserable.

The bitterest misery was yet to come. It came in the person of a certain Captain George Duke, who dropped into Compton on his way from Marley Water to the metropolis, and who contrived to scrape acquaintance with Squire Markham in the best parlor at the Black Bear. Captain George and Master Ringwood became sworn friends in a day or two, and the hearty sailor promised to stop at Compton again on his return to his ship, the *Vulture*.

The simple villagers readily accepted Captain Duke as that which he represented himself, an officer of His Majesty's navy; but there were people in the seaport of Marley Water who said that the good ship whose name was written down as the *Vulture* in the Admiralty's books was quite a different class of vessel, to the trim little craft which lay sometimes in a quiet corner of the obscure harbor at Marley. There were malicious people who whispered such words as 'privateer!—pirate!—slaver!'—but the most daring took good care only to whisper out of the Captain's hearing, for George Duke's sword was as often out of its scabbard as in it during his brief visits to the little seaport. However it might be, handsome, rollicking, light-hearted, free-handed George Duke became a great favorite with Squire Markham and his son Ringwood.

Compton Hall rang night after night with the gay peals of his hearty laughter; corks flew, and glasses jingled, as the three men sat up till midnight (a terrible hour at Compton) over their Burgundy and claret. It was in one of these half-drunken bouts that Squire Markham promised the hand of his daughter Millicent to Captain George Duke.

'You're in love with her, George, and you shall have her!' the old man said; 'I can give her a couple of thousand pounds at my death, and if anything should happen to Ringwood, she'll be sole heiress to the Compton property. You shall have her, my boy! I know there's some sneaking courtship been going on between Milly and a broad-shouldered, fair-haired nephew of mine, but that shan't stand in your way, for the lad is no favorite with me; and if I choose to say it, my fine lack-a-daisical miss shall marry you in a week's time.'

Captain Duke sprang from his chair, and wringing the squire's hand in his, cried out with a lover's rapture—

'She's the prettiest girl in England! and I'd sooner have her than any duchess at St. James's.'

'She's pretty enough as for that,' said Ringwood, superciliously, 'and she'd be a deal prettier if she was not always whimpering.'

Farmer Morrison could have told how Master Ringwood himself had gone whimpering out of the sanded kitchen on the day that Darrell Markham knocked him down; and the plain-spoken farmer told him, after dressing his broken head, that if he ever came about those premises again, it would be to get such a thrashing as he would be easily able to remember.

Both the children inherited something of the nervous weakness of that poor, delicate, and neglected mother who had died seventeen years before in Sally Masterson's arms; but timid and sensitive as Millicent was, I think that the higher nature had been given to her, and that beneath that childish timidity and that nervous excitability which would bring tears into her eyes at the sound of a harsh word, there was a latent and quiet courage that had no existence in Ringwood's selfish and frivolous character.

Harsh words on this occasion, as on every other, did their work with Millicent Markham. She heard her father's determination that she should marry George Duke, at first, with a stupid apathetic stare, as if the calamity were too great for her to realize its misery at one grasp; then, as he repeated his command, her clear blue eyes brimmed over with big tears, as she fell on her knees at his feet.

'You don't mean it, sir,' she said, piteously clasping her poor little feeble hands. 'You know that I love my cousin Darrell, and that we are to be man and wife when you are pleased to give your consent. You must have known it all along, sir, though we had not the courage to tell you. I will be your obedient child in everything but this; but I never, never can marry any one but Darrell!'

What need to tell the old story of stupid, obstinate, narrow-minded country squire's fury and tyranny. Did not poor Sophia Western suffer all these torments, though in the dear old romance all is so happily settled in the last chapter; but in this case it was different—Squire Markham would hear of no delay; and before Darrell could get the letter which Millicent addressed to a coffee-house near Covent Garden, and bribed one of the servants to give to the Compton post-master—before the eyes of the bride had recovered from long nights of weeping—before the village had half discussed the matter—before Mrs. Sarah Pecker could finish the petticoat she was quilting for the bride—the bells of Compton church were ringing a cheery peal in the morning sunshine, and Millicent Markham and George Duke were standing side by side at the altar.

When Darrell Markham received the poor little tear-stained letter, telling him of this ill-omened marriage, he fell into an outburst of rage; an outburst of blind fury which swept alike upon the squire, young Ringwood, Captain George Duke, and even poor Millicent herself. It is so difficult for a man to understand the influence brought to bear upon a weak, helpless woman by the tyranny of a brutal father. Darrell cried out passionately that Millicent ought to have been true to him, in spite of the whole world, as he would have been to her, through every trial. Made desperate by the shipwreck of his happiness, he rushed for a brief period into the dissipations of the town, and tried to drown Millicent's fair face in tavern measures and long draughts of Burgundy.

A marriage contracted under such circumstances was not likely to be a very happy one. Light-hearted, rollicking George Duke was by no means a delightful person by the domestic hearth. At home he was moody and ill-tempered, always ready to grumble at Millicent's pale face, and tear-swollen eyes. For the best part of the year he was away with his ship, on some of those mysterious voyages of which the Admiralty knew so little; and in these long absences, Millicent, if not happy, was at least at rest. Three months after the wedding the old squire was found dead in his arm-chair, and Ringwood succeeding to the estate, shut up the Hall, and rushed away to London, where he was soon lost to the honest folks of Compton in a whirlpool of vice and dissipation.

This was how matters stood when George and Millicent had been married fifteen months, and Darrell Markham well-nigh lost his life upon the dreary moorland road to Marley Water.

CHAPTER IV.—CAPTAIN DUKE PROVES AN ALIBI.

Darrell Markham did not die from the effects of that excitement which the doctor said might be so fatal. He was very slow to recover; so slow that the snow lay white upon the moorland before the windows of the Black Bear, before the shattered arm was firmly knit together, or the enfeebled frame restored to its native vigor. It was a dreary and tedious illness. Honest Sarah Pecker was nearly worn out with nursing her sick boy, as she insisted on calling Darrell. The weak-eyed Samuel was made to wear list shoes and to creep like a thief about his roomy hostelry. The evening visitors were sent into a dark tap-room at the back of the house, that the sound of their revelry might not disturb the sick man. Gloom and sadness reigned in the Black Bear until that happy day upon which. Doctor Jordan pronounced his patient to be out of danger. Sarah Pecker gave away a barrel of the strongest ale upon that joyous afternoon, giving freely to every loiterer who stopped to ask after poor Maister Darrell

Captain George Duke was away ou a brief voyage round the Spanish coast, when Darrell began to mend; but by the time the young man had completely re-covered, the sailor returned to Compton.

The snow was thick in the narrow street when the Captain came back. He found Millicent sitting in her old attitude by the fire, reading a novel.

But he was in a better temper than usual, and looked wonderfully handsome and dashing in his weather-beaten uniform. Not quite the King's uniform, as some people said; very like it, but yet with slight technical differences, that told against the Captain.

He caught Millicent in his arms, and gave her a hearty kiss upon each cheek, before he had time to notice the faint repellant shudder.

'I've come home to you laden with good things, Mistress Milly,' he said, as he seated himself opposite to her, while the stout servant-maid piled fresh logs upon the blazing fire. 'A chest of oranges, and a cask of wine from Cadiz—liquid gold, my girl, and almost as precious as the sterling metal; and I've a heap of pretty barbarous trumpery for you to fasten on your white neck and arms, and hang in your rosy little ears.' The Captain took an old-fashioned, queerly shaped leather case from his pocket, and opening it, spread out a quantity of foreign jew-elry, that glittered and twinkled in the fire-light. Arabesqued gold of wonderful workmanship, and strange, outlandish, many-colored gems sparkled upon the dark oak table, and reflected themselves deep down in the polished wood, like stars in a river.

Millicent blushed as she bent over the trinkets, and stammered out some gen-tle, grateful phrases. She was blushing to think how little she cared for all these gew-gaws, and how her soul was set on other treasures which never could be—the treasures of Darrell's deep and honest love.

As she was thinking this, the Captain looked up at her carelessly, as it seemed, but in reality, with a very searching glance in his flashing brown eyes.

'Oh, by-the-bye,' he said, 'how is that pretty fair-haired cousin of yours? Has he recovered from that affair? or was it his death?'

There was a malicious sparkle in his eyes, as he watched her shiver at that cruel word, Death.

'That's another figure in the long score between you and I, my lady,' he thought.

'He is much better. Indeed, he is nearly well,' Millicent said, quietly.

'Have you seen him?'

'Never since the night on which you found me at his bedside.'

She looked up at him calmly, almost proudly, as she spoke. It was a look that seemed to say, 'I have a clear conscience, and do what you will, you cannot make me blush or falter.'

She had indeed a clear conscience. Many times Sarah Pecker had come to her and said, 'Your cousin is very low to-night, Miss Millicent; come and sit beside him, if it's only for half an hour, to cheer him up a bit. Poor old Sally will be with you, and where she is, the hardest can't say there's harm.'

But Millicent had always steadily refused, saying, 'It would only make us both unhappy, Sally dear. I'd rather not come.'

None knew how, sometimes late at night, when the maid-servant had gone to bed, and the lights in the upper windows of Compton High Street had been one by one extinguished, this same inflexible Millicent would steal out, muffled in a long cloak of shadowy grey, and creep to the roadway under the Black Bear, to stand for ten minutes in the snow and rain, watching the faint light that shone from the window of the room where Darrell Markham lay.

Once, standing ankle-deep in snow, she saw Sarah Pecker open the window to look out at the night, and heard his voice, faint in the distance, asking if it were snowing.

She burst into tears at the sound of this feeble voice. It seemed so long since she had heard it, she fancied she might never hear it again.

One of the *Vulture's* men brought the case of oranges and the cask of sherry from Marley to Compton upon the very night of the Captain's return, and George Duke drank half a bottle of the liquid gold before he went to bed. He tried in vain to induce Millicent to taste the topaz-colored liquor. She liked Sarah Pecker's cowslip wine better than the finest sherry ever grown in the Peninsula.

Early the next morning the Compton constable came to the cottage armed with a warrant for the apprehension of Captain George Duke, on a charge of assault and robbery on the King's highway. Pale with suppressed fury, the Captain strode into the little parlour where Millicent was seated at breakfast.

'Pray, Mistress Millicent,' he said, 'who has set on your pretty cousin to try and hang an innocent man, with the intent to make a hempen widow of you, as I suppose? What is the meaning of this?'

'Of what, George?' she asked, bewildered by his manner.

He told her the whole story of the warrant. 'Of course,' he said, 'you remember this Master Darrell's crying out it was I who shot him?'

'I do, George; I thought then it was some strange feverish delusion, and I think so now.'

'I scarcely expected so much of your courtesy, Mistress Duke,' answered her husband. 'Luckily for me, I can pretty easily clear myself from this mad-brained charge, but I'm not the less grateful to Darrell Markham for his kind intent.'

They took Captain Duke at once to the magistrate's parlour, where he found Darrell Markham seated, pale from his long illness, and with his arm still in a sling.

'Thank you, Mr. Markham, for this good turn,' said the Captain, folding his arms and placing himself against the doorway of the magistrate's room; 'we shall find an opportunity of squaring our accounts, I dare say.'

The worthy magistrate was not a little puzzled as to how to deal with the case before him. Little as was known in Compton of Captain George Duke, it seemed incredible that the husband of Squire Markham's daughter could be guilty of highway robbery.

Darrell stated his charge in the simplest and most straightforward fashion. He had ridden away from the Black Bear to go to Marley Water. Three miles from Compton, a man, whom he swore to as the accused, rode up to him and demanded his purse and watch. He drew his pistol from his belt, but while he was cocking it, the man, Captain Duke, fired, shot him in the arm, and dragging him off his horse, threw him into the mud. He remembered nothing more until he awoke in the hall at the Black Bear, and recognized the accused amongst the bystanders.

The magistrate coughed dubiously.

'Cases of mistaken identity have not been uncommon in the judicial history of this country,' he said sententiously. 'Can you swear, Mr. Markham, that the man who attacked you was Captain George Duke?'

'If that man standing against the door is Captain Duke, I can solemnly swear that he is the man who robbed me.'

'When you were found by the persons who picked you up, was your horse found also?'

'No; the horse was gone.'

'Would you know him again?'

'Know him again? What, honest Balmerino? I should know him amongst a thousand.'

'Hum!' said the magistrate; 'that is a great point; I consider the horse a great point.'

He pondered so long over this very important part of the case that his clerk had to nudge him respectfully, and whisper something in his ear before he went on again.

'Oh, ah, yes, to be sure, of course,' he muttered, helplessly; then, clearing his throat, he said, in his magisterial voice, 'Pray, Captain Duke, what have you to say to this charge?'

'Very little,' said the Captain, quietly; 'but before I speak at all, I should be glad if you would send for Mr. Samuel Pecker, of the Black Bear.'

The magistrate whispered to the clerk, and the clerk nodded, on which the magistrate said, 'Go, one of you, and fetch the aforesaid Samuel Pecker.'

While one of the hangers-on was gone upon this errand, the worthy magistrate nodded over his *Flying Post*, the clerk mended the fire, and Mr. Darrell Markham and the Captain stared fiercely at each other—an ominous red glimmer burning in the sailor's brown eyes.

Mr. Pecker came with a white face and limp, disordered hair, to attend the magisterial summons. He had some vague idea that hanging might be the result of this morning's work; or that, happily escaping that, he would suffer a hundred moral deaths at the hands of Sarah, his wife. He could not for a moment imagine that he could possibly be wanted in the magistrate's parlour, unless accused of some monstrous, though unconsciously-committed crime.

He gave a faint gasp of relief when some one in the room whispered to him that he was required as a witness.

'Now, Captain Duke,' said the magistrate, 'what have you to say to this?'

'Will you be good enough to ask Mr. Darrell Markham two or three questions?'

The magistrate looked at the clerk, the clerk nodded to the magistrate, and the magistrate nodded an assent to Captain Duke's request.

'Will you ask if he knows at what time the assault was committed?'

Before the magistrate could interpose, Darrell Markham spoke—

'I happen to be able to answer that question with certainty,' he said. 'The wind was blowing straight across the moor, and I distinctly heard Compton church clock chime the three-quarters after seven as the man rode up to me.'

'As I rode up to you?' asked George Duke.

'As *you* rode up to me,' answered Darrell.

'Mr. Samuel Pecker, will you be so good as to tell the magistrate where I was at a quarter to eight o'clock upon the night of the 27th of October?'

'You were in the parlour at the Bear, Captain,' answered Samuel, in short gasps; 'and you come in and ask the time, which I went out to look at our eight-day on the stairs, it were ten minutes to eight exact by father's eight day, as is never a minute wrong.'

'There were other people in the parlour that night who saw me and who heard me ask the question, were there not, Mr. Pecker?'

'There were a many of 'em,' replied Samuel; 'which they saw you wind your watch by father's eight-day; for it weren't you, Captain Duke, as robbed Master Darrell, but *I* know who it were.'

There was stupefaction in the court at this extraordinary assertion.

'You know!' cried the magistrate; 'then, pray, why have you withheld the knowledge from those entitled to hear it? This is very bad, Mr. Pecker; very bad, indeed!'

The unhappy Samuel felt that he was in for it.

'It were no more Captain Duke than it were me,' he gasped; 'it were the other.'

'The other! What other?'

'Him as stopped his horse at the door of the Black Bear, and asked the way to Marley Water.'

Nothing could remove Samuel Pecker from this position. Questioned and cross-questioned by the magistrate, the clerk, and Darrell Markham, he steadfastly declared that a man so closely resembling Captain Duke as to deceive both himself and John Homerton, the blacksmith, had stopped at the Black Bear, and asked the way to Marley.

He gasped and stuttered and choked and bewildered himself, but he neither prevaricated nor broke down in his assertions, and he begged that John Homerton might be summoned to confirm his statement.

John Homerton was summoned, and declared that to the best of his belief, it was Captain Duke who stopped at the Black Bear, while he, Master Darrell Markham, and the landlord were standing at the door.

But this assertion was shivered in a moment by an *alibi*. A quarter of an hour after the traveller had ridden off towards Marley, Captain Duke walked up to the inn from the direction of the High Street.

Neither the magistrate nor the clerk had anything to say to this. The affair seemed altogether in a mystery, for which the legal experience of the Compton worthies could furnish no parallel.

If James Dobbs assaulted Farmer Hobbs, it was easy to deal with him according to the precedent afforded by the celebrated case of Jones *vs.* Smith; but the affair of to-day stood alone in the judicial records of Compton.

While the magistrate and his factotum consulted together in a whisper, without getting any nearer to a decision, George Duke himself came to their rescue.

'I suppose after the charge having broken down in this manner, I need not stop here any longer, sir,' he said.

The magistrate caught at this chance of extrication.

'The charge *has* broken down,' he said, with solemn importance, 'and, as you observe, Captain Duke, and as indeed I was about to observe myself, we need not detain you any longer. You leave this room with as good a character as that with which you entered it,' he added, while a slight titter circulated among some of the bystanders at this rather ambiguous compliment. 'I am sorry, Mr. Markham, that this affair is so involved in mystery. It is evidently a case of mistaken identity, one of the most difficult class of cases that the law ever has to deal with; but, as I said before, I consider the missing horse a great point—a very strong point.'

The Captain and Darrell Markham left the room at the same time.

'I have an account to settle with you, Mr. Markham, for this morning's work,' Captain Duke whispered to his accuser.

'I do not fight with highwaymen,' Darrell answered, proudly.

'What, you still dare to insinuate —— ?'

'I dare to say that I don't believe in this story of George Duke and his double. I believe that you proved an *alibi* by some juggling with the clock at the Black Bear, and I most firmly believe that you are the man who shot me!'

'You shall pay for this,' hissed the Captain, through his set teeth; 'you shall pay double for every insolent word, Darrell Markham, before you and I have done with each other.'

He strode away, after flinging one dark, wicked look at his wife's cousin, and returned to the cottage where Millicent, pale and anxious, was awaiting the result of the morning.

Darrell Markham left Compton by the mail coach that very night; and poorer by the loss of his horse, his watch, and purse, set forth once more to seek his fortune in cruel, stony-hearted London.

CHAPTER V.—MILLICENT MEETS HER HUSBAND'S SHADOW.

A fortnight after Darrell's departure, the good ship *Vulture* was nearly ready for another cruise, and Captain Duke rode off to Marley Water to superintend the final preparations.

'I shall sail on the thirtieth, Milly,' he said, the day he left Compton, ' and as I shan't have time to ride over here and say good-bye to you, I should like you to come to Marley, and see me before I start.'

'I will come, if you wish, George,' she answered, quietly. She was always gentle and obedient, something as a child might have been to a hard taskmaster, but in no way like a wife who loved her husband.

'Very good. There's a branch coach passes through here three times a week from York to Carlisle; it stops at Marley Water. You can come by that, Millicent.'

'Yes, George.'

The snow never melted upon Compton Moor throughout the dark January days. Millicent felt a strange, dull aching at her heart as she stood before the door of the Black Bear waiting for the Carlisle coach, and watching the dreary expanse of glistening white that stretched far away to the dark horizon. She had seen it often under the tenantless moonlight when Darrell Markham was lying on his sick bed. Dismal as that sad time had been, she looked back on it with a sigh. He was near her then, she thought, and now he was lost in the wild vortex of terrible London—lost to her, perhaps, forever.

Mrs Sarah Pecker cried out indignantly at this wintry journey.

'What does the Captain mean by it,' she said, ' sending off a poor delicate lamb like you four-and-twenty mile in a old fusty stage-coach upon such a afternoon as this. If he wants you to catch your death, Miss Milly, he's a-going the right way to bring about his wicked wishes.'

The great, heavy, lumbering, broad-shouldered coach drove up while Mistress Pecker was still holding forth upon this subject. One or two of the inside passengers looked out and asked for brandy-and-water while the horses were being changed. Some of the outsides clambered down from the roof of the vehicle, and went into the Black Bear to warm themselves at the blazing fire in the parlour and drink a glass of raw spirits. One man seated upon the box refused to alight, when asked to do so by another passenger, and sat with his face turned away from the inn, looking straight out upon the snowy moorland.

If even this man's face had been turned towards the little group at the door of the Black Bear, they would have had considerable difficulty in distinguishing his features, for he wore his three-cornered hat slouched over his eyes, and the collar of his thick horseman's coat drawn close up to his ears.

'He's a grim customer up yonder,' said the man who had spoken to this outside passenger, designating him by a jerk of the head—' a regular grim customer. I wonder what he is, and where he's going to.'

Mistress Pecker assisted Millicent into the coach, settled her in a warm corner, and wrapped her camlet cloak about her.

'You'd better have one of Samuel's comforters for your throat, Miss Milly,' she said, 'and one of his coats to wrap about your feet. Its bitter weather for such a journey.'

Millicent declined the coat and the comforter; but she kissed her old nurse as the coachman drew his horses together for the start.

'God bless you, Sally.' she said; 'I wish the journey was over and done with, and that I was back again with you.'

The coach drove off before Mrs. Pecker could answer.

'Poor dear child,' said the inn-keeper's wife, 'to think of her going out alone and friendless on such a day as this. She wishes she was back with us, she said. I sometimes think there's a look in her poor mournful blue eyes, as if she wished she was lying quiet and calm in Compton churchyard.'

The high-road from Compton to Marley Water wound amongst bleak and sterile moors, passing now and then a long straggling village or a lonely farm-house. It was longer by this road than by the moorland bridle path, and it was quite dark when the stage coach drove over the uneven pavement of the high-street of Marley Water.

Millicent found her husband waiting for her at the inn where the coach stopped.

'You're just in time, Milly,' he said; 'the *Vulture* sails to-night.'

Captain Duke was stopping at a tavern on the quay. He put Millicent's arm in his, and led her through the narrow high-street.

This Principal street of Marley Water was lighted here and there by feeble oil-lamps, which shed a wan light upon the figures of the foot-passengers.

Glancing behind her, once, bewildered by the strange bustle of the busy little seaport town, Millicent was surprised to see the outside passenger whom she had observed at Compton, following close upon their heels.

Captain Duke felt the little hand tighten upon his arm with a nervous shiver.

'What made you start?' he asked.

'The—the man!'

'What man?'

'A man who traveled outside the coach, and whose face was quite concealed by his hat and cloak. He is just behind us.'

George Duke looked back, but the outside passenger was no longer to be seen.

'What a silly child you are, Millicent,' he said. 'What is there so wonderful in your seeing one of your fellow-passengers in the high-street ten minutes after the coach has stopped?'

'But he seemed to be following us.'

'Why, my country wench, people walk close behind each other in busy towns without any such thought as following their neighbors. Millicent. Millicent, when will you learn to be wise?'

The Captain of the *Vulture* seemed in unusually good spirits this late January night.

'I shall be far away upon the blue water in twenty-four hours, Milly,' he said. 'No one but a sailor can tell a sailor's weariness of land.' I heard of your brother Ringwood last night.'

'Bad news?' asked Millicent anxiously.

'No; good news for you, who will come in for his money if he dies unmarried. He's leading a wild life, and wasting his substance in taverns, and worse places than taverns. Luckily for the boy, Compton property is safely secured, so that he can neither sell nor mortgage it.'

The little inn at which George Duke was stopping faced the water, and Millicent could see the lights on board the *Vulture*, gleaming far away through the winter night, from the window of the little parlor where supper was laid out ready for the traveller.

'At what o'clock do you sail, George?' she asked.

'A little before midnight. You can go down to the pier with me, and see the last of me, and you can get back to Compton by the return coach to-morrow morning.'

'I will do exactly as you please. Will this voyage be a long one, George?'

'Not long. I shall be back in three months at the latest.'

Her heart sank at his ready answer. She was always so much happier in his absence. Happy in her trim little cottage, her stout, good-tempered servants, the friends who had known her from her childhood, her novels, her old companion, the faithful brown and white spaniel—happy in all these—happy, too, in her undisturbed memories of Darrell Markham.

While George and his wife were seated at the little supper-table, one of the servants of the inn came to say that Captain Duke was wanted.

'Who wants me?' he asked, impatiently.

'A man wrapped in a horseman's coat, and with his hat over his eyes, Captain.'

'Did you tell him that I was busy; that I was just going to sail?'

'I did, Captain; but he says that he must see you. He has traveled above two hundred miles on purpose.'

An angry darkness spread itself over the Captain's handsome face.

'Curse such interruption,' he said, savagely. 'Let him come up stairs. Here, Millicent,' he added, when the waiter had left the room, 'take one of those candles, and go into the opposite chamber; it is my sleeping room. Quick, girl, quick.'

He thrust the candlestick into her hand with an impatient gesture, and almost pushed her out of the room in his flurry and agitation.

She hurried across the landing-place into the opposite chamber, but not before she had recognized in the man ascending the stairs the outside passenger who had followed them in the high-street; not before she had heard her husband say, as he shut the parlour door upon himself and his visitor—

'You here! By heaven, I guessed as much.'

Some logs burned upon the open hearth in the Captain's bed-room, and Millicent seated herself on a low stool before the warm blaze. She sat for upwards of an hour wondering at this stranger's lengthened interview with her husband. Once she went on to the landing to see if the visitor had left. She heard the voices of the two men raised as if in anger, but she could not hear their words.

The clock was striking eleven as the parlour door opened and the stranger descended the stairs. Captain Duke crossed the landing-place and looked into the bed-room where Millicent sat brooding over the fire.

'Come,' he said, 'I have little better than half an hour to get off; put on your cloak and come with me.'

It was a bitter cold night, but the moon was nearly at the full, and shone upon the stone pier and the white quays with a cold, steely light, that gave a ghostly

3

brightness to every object upon which it fell. The outlines of the old-fashioned houses along the quay were cut black and sharp against this blue light; every coil of rope and idle anchor, every bag of ballast lying upon the edge of the parapet, every chain and post, and iron ring attached to the solid masonry, was visible in this winter moonlight. The last brawlers had left the tavern on the quay, the last stragglers had deserted the narrow streets, the last dim lights had been extinguished in the upper windows, and Marley Water, at a little after eleven o'clock, was as still as the quiet churchyard at Compton-on-the-Moor.

Millicent shivered as she walked by her husband's side along the main quay; once or twice she glanced at him furtively; she could see the sharp lines of his profile against the purple atmosphere, and she could see by his face that he had some trouble on his mind. They turned off the quay on to the pier which stretched far out into the water.

'The boat is to wait for me at the other end,' said Captain Duke. 'The tide has turned, and the wind is in our favour.'

He walked for some time in silence, Millicent watching him timidly all the while; presently he turned to her, and said, abruptly—

'Mistress George Duke, have you a ring or any such foolish trinket about you?'

'A ring, George?' she said, bewildered by the suddenness of the question.

'A ring, a brooch, a locket, a ribbon, anything which you could swear to twenty years hence if need were.'

She had a locket hanging about her throat which had been given to her by Darrell, than which she would have sooner parted with her life.

'A locket?' she said, hesitating.

'Anything! Haven't I said before, anything?'

'I have the little diamond ear-rings in my ears, George.'

'Give me one of them, then; I have a fancy to take some token of you with me on my voyage. The ear-ring will do.'

She took the jewel from her ear and handed it to him. She was too indifferent to him and to all things in her weary life even to wonder at his motive in asking for the trinket.

'This is better than anything, Millicent,' he said, slipping the jewel into his waistcoat pocket; 'the ear-rings are of Indian workmanship, and of a rare pattern. Remember, Millicent, the man who comes to you and calls himself your husband, yet cannot give you this diamond ear-ring, will not be George Duke.'

'What do you mean, George?'

'When I return to Compton, ask me for the fellow jewel to that in your ear. If I cannot show it to you——'

'What then, George?'

'Drive me from your door as an impostor.'

'But you may lose it.'

'I shall not lose it.'

He relapsed into silence. They walked on towards the farther end of the long pier, their shadows stretching out before them black upon the moonlit stones.

They were half a mile from the quay, and they were alone upon the pier, with no sound to wake the silence but the echoes of their own footsteps and the noise of the waves dashing against the stone bulwarks.

The *Vulture's* boat was waiting at the end of the pier. Captain George Duke took his wife in his arms and pressed his lips to her cold forehead.

'You will have a lonely walk back to the inn, Millicent,' he said; 'but I have told them to make you comfortable; and to see you safely off by the return coach to-morrow morning. Good-bye, and God bless you. Remember what I have told you to-night.'

Something in his manner—a tenderness that was strange to him—touched her gentle heart.

She stopped him as he was about to descend the steps.

'It has been my unhappiness that I have never been a good wife to you, George Duke. I will pray for your safety while you are far away upon the cruel sea.'

The Captain pressed her trembling little hand.

'Good-bye, Millicent,' he said, 'and remember.'

Before she could answer him he was gone. She saw the men push the boat off from the steps; she heard the regular strokes of the oars plashing through the water, the little craft skimming lightly over the surface of the waves.

He was gone; she could return to her quiet cottage at Compton, her novel reading, her old friends, her undisturbed recollections of Darrell Markham.

She stood watching the boat till it grew into a dim, black speck upon the moonlit waters; then she slowly turned and walked towards the quay.

A long, lonely walk at that dead hour of the night for such a delicately nurtured woman as Millicent Duke! She was not a courageous woman either; rather over-sensitive and nervous, as the reader knows; fond of reading silly romances, such as people wrote a century ago, full of mysteries and horrors, of haunted chambers, secret passages, midnight encounters, and masked assassins.

The clocks of Marley Water began to strike twelve as she approached the centre of the desolate pier. One by one, the different iron voices slowly rang out the hour; smaller voices in the distance taking up the sound, and all Marley and all the sea, to her fancy, tremulous with the sonorous vibration. As the last stroke from the last clock died away and the sleeping town relapsed into silence, she heard the noise of a man's footstep slowly approaching her.

She must meet him and pass by him in order to reach the quay.

She had a strange vague fear of this encounter. He might be a highwayman, he might attack and attempt to rob her.

The poor girl was prepared to throw her purse and all her little trinkets at his feet—all but Darrell's locket.

Still the footsteps slowly approached. The stranger came nearer and nearer in the ghastly moonlight—nearer, until he came face to face with Millicent Duke.

Then she stopped. She meant to have hurried by the man, to have avoided even being seen by him, if possible. But she stood face to face with him, rooted to the ground, a heavy languor paralysing her limbs, an unearthly chill creeping to the very roots of her hair.

Her hands fell powerless at her sides. She could only stand, white and immovable, with dilated eyes, staring blankly into the man's face. He wore a blue coat, and a three-cornered hat, thrown jauntily upon his head, so as in nowise to overshadow his face.

She was alone, half a mile from a human habitation or human help—alone at the stroke of midnight, with her husband's ghost.

There was no illusion; no shadowy deception, save of a fervid imagination. There, line for line, shade for shade, stood a shadow who wore the outward seeming of George Duke.

She reeled away from him, tottered feebly forward for a few faces, and then summoning a desperate courage, rushed blindly on towards the quay, her garments fluttering in the sharp winter air. She reached the inn; a servant had waited up to receive her; the sea-coal fire burned brightly in the wainscoted little sitting-room; all within was cheerful and pleasant.

Millicent fell into the girl's arms and sobbed aloud. 'Don't leave me,' she said; 'don't leave me alone this terrible night. I have often heard that such things were, but never knew before how truly people spoke who told of them. This will be a bad voyage for the ship that sails to-night. I have seen my husband's ghost.'

CHAPTER VI.—SALLY PECKER LIFTS THE CURTAIN OF THE PAST.

The best part of the year had dragged out its slow monotonous course since that moonlit January night upon which Millicent Duke had stood face to face with the shadow of her husband upon the long stone pier at Marley Water. The story of Captain George Duke's ghost was pretty well known in the quiet village of Compton-on-the-Moor, though Millicent had only told it under the seal of secresy to honest Sally Pecker.

We are but mortal. Mrs. Sally Pecker had tried to keep this solemn secret, but her very reticence was so overstrained, that in three days all Compton knew that the hostess at the Black Bear had something wonderful on her mind which she 'could, an' if she would,' reveal to her especial friends and customers.

Again, though Millicent might be sole proprietress of that midnight encounter at Marley, had not Samuel Pecker himself a prior claim upon the Captain's ghost? Had he not seen and conversed with the apparition? 'I see him as plain, Sarah, as I see the oven and the spit as I'm sitting before at this present time,' Samuel protested. It was but natural, then, that, little by little, dark hints of the mystery oozed out, and that when the three months appointed for the voyage of the *Vulture* expired, and Captain Duke did not return to Compton, the honest Cumbrians began to look solemnly at each other and to mutter ominously that they had never looked to see George Duke touch British ground alive.

But Millicent heard none of these whispers; shut up in her cottage, she read the well-thumbed romances, sitting in the high-backed arm chair, with the white and brown spaniel at her feet, and Darrell Markham's locket in her bosom. The stout servant girl went out in the evenings now and then, and heard the Compton gossip; but if ever she thought of repeating it to her mistress, she felt the words die away upon her lips as she looked at Millicent's pale face and mournful blue eyes.

'Madam has trouble enough,' she thought, 'without hearing their talk.' It seemed, as month after month passed away—as the long grass grew deep in the meadow round Compton, and fell in rich waves of dewy green under the mower's scythe—as the stackers spread their smooth straw thatch over groups of noble hayricks clustering about the farm houses—as the corn began to change color, and yellow shades came slowly creeping up the waving stalks towards the heavy ears of wheat and rye—as the ponderous wagons staggered homewards under their rich burdens of golden store—as the flat stubborn fields were laid bare to the autumn breezes, and the ripening blackberries grew black in the hedges—as the bright foliage in the woods slowly faded out, and the withered leaves rustled to the ground—as the early frost began to sparkle upon the whitened moors in the chilly sunrise—as the pale November fog came stealing over the wide moorland, and creeping into Compton High street in the early twilight—as Time, with every changing sign with which he marks his course upon the face of nature, passed away, and still no tidings of Captain George Duke and the good ship *Vulture* were heard in Compton;—it seemed, I say, as if the honest villagers had indeed been strangely near the truth when they said that the Captain would never touch British ground again. In all Compton, Millicent Duke was, perhaps, the only person who thought differently.

'It is but ten months that he has been away,' she said, when Mrs. Sally Pecker hinted to her that the chances seemed to be against the Captain's return, and that it might be only correct were she to think of putting on mourning, 'it is not ten months; and George Duke was never an over anxious husband. If it seemed pleasant or profitable to him to stay away, no thought of me would bring him back any the sooner. If it was three years, Sally, I should think little of it, and expect any day to see him walk into the cottage.'

'Him as you saw upon the pier at Marley, perhaps, Miss Milly,' answered Sally, solemnly, 'but not Captain Duke. Such things as you and Samuel see last winter arn't shown to folks for nothing, and it seems like doubting Providence after that to doubt that the Captain's been drowned. I dreamt three times that I see my first husband, Thomas Masterson, lying dead upon a bit of rock in the middle of a stormy sea; and I put on widow's weeds after the third time.'

'But you had news of his death, Sally, hadn't you.'

'No more news than his staying away seventeen year and more, Miss Milly, and if that ain't news enough to make a woman a widow, I don't know what is!'

Millicent was sitting on a low stool at Mrs. Sally Pecker's feet before a cheerful sea-coal fire in the snug little parlor at the Black Bear. It was a comfort to the poor girl to spend these long wintry evenings with honest Sally, listening to the wind roaring in the wide chimneys, counting the drops of rain beating against the window panes, and talking of the dear old times that were past and gone.

The customers at the Black Bear were a very steady set of people, who came and went at the same hours, and ordered the same things from year's end to year's end; so when Sally had her dear young mistress to visit her, she left the feeble Samuel to entertain and wait upon his patrons, and, turning her back to business and the bar, took gentle Millicent's pale golden head upon her knee, and lovingly smoothing the soft curls, comforted the forlorn heart with that talk of the days gone by that was so mournfully sweet to Mistress George Duke.

Long as Sarah Masterson had been housekeeper at the Hall, Millicent never remembered having heard any mention whatever of the name of Thomas Masterson, mariner; but on this dark November evening some chance word brought Sarah's first husband into Mrs. Duke's thoughts, and she felt a strange curiosity about the dead seaman.

'Was he good to you, Sally?' she asked, 'and did you love him?'

Sally looked gloomily at the fire for some moments before she answered this question.

'It's a long while ago, Miss Millicent,' she said, 'and it seems hard, looking back so far, to remember what was and what wasn't. I was but a poor stupid lass when Masterson first came to Compton. I did love him, Miss Milly, and he warn't good to me.'

'Not good to you, Sally?'

'He was bitter, bad and cruel to me,' answered Sally in a suppressed voice, her eyes kindling at the angry recollection. 'I had a bit of money left me by poor old grandfather, and it was that he wanted, and not me. I had a few bits of silver spoons and a teapot as had been grandmother's, and he cared more for them than me. I had my savings that I had been keeping ever since I first went to service, and he wrung every guinea from me, and every crownpiece, and shilling, and copper, till he left me without clothes to cover me, and almost without bread to eat. You see me here, Miss, with Samuel, having my own way in everything, and managing of him mild like. You wouldn't believe I was the same woman, if you'd seen me with Masterson. I was frightened of him, Miss Millicent!—I was frightened of him.'

The very recollection of her dead husband seemed to strike terror to the stout heart of the ponderous Sally Pecker. She cowered down over the fire, clinging to Millicent as if she would have turned for protection even to that slender reed, and, glancing across her shoulder, looked towards the window behind her, as if she expected to see it shaken by some more terrible touch than that of the wind and rain.

'Sally, Sally!' exclaimed Millicent soothingly, for it was now her turn to be the comforter, 'why were you frightened of him?'

'Because he was—— I haven't told you all the truth about him yet, Miss Millicent, and I've never told it to mortal ears, and never will except to yours. I've called him a mariner, Miss, for this seventeen years and past. It's not a hard word, and it means almost anything in the way of sailoring; but he was one of the most desperate smugglers as ever robbed king and country, and I found it out three months after we was married.'

It was some little time before Millicent uttered a word in reply to this. She sat with her slender hands clasped round one of Sarah's plump wrists, her large blue eyes fixed upon the red blaze with the thoughtfully earnest gaze peculiar to her.

'My poor, poor Sally! it was very hard for you,' she said at last. 'Compton seems so far away from the world, and we so ignorant, that it was little wonder you were deceived. Others have been deceived, Sally, since then.'

Mrs. Sarah Pecker nodded her head. She had heard the dark reports current among the Compton people about the good ship *Vulture* and her captain. She only sighed thoughtfully, as she murmured—

'Ah, Miss Milly, if that had been the worst, I might have borne it uncomplainingly, for I was milder tempered those days than I am now. We didn't live at Compton, but in a little village along the coast, as was handy for my husband's unlawful trade. We'd lived together five years, me never daring to complain of any hardships, nor of the wickedness of cheating the king as Thomas Masterson cheated him every week of his life. I seemed not much to care what he did, or where he went, for I had my comfort and my happiness. I had my boy, who was born a year after we left Compton—my beautiful boy, with the great black eyes and the curly hair—and I was as happy as the day was long while all went well with him. But the bitterest was to come, Miss Milly, for when the child came to be four years old, I saw that the father was teaching him his own bad ways, and putting his own wicked words into the baby's innocent mouth, and bringing him up in a fair way to be a curse to himself and them that loved him. I couldn't bear this; I could have borne to have been trampled on myself, but I couldn't bear to see my child going to ruin before his mother's eyes. I told Masterson so one night. I was violent, perhaps, for I was almost wild like, and my passion carried me away. I told him that I meant to take the child away with me out of his reach, and go into service and work for him, and bring him up to be an honest man. He laughed and said I was welcome to the brat, and I took him at his word, thinking he didn't care. I went to sleep with the boy in my arms, meaning to set out early the next morning, and come back to Compton, where I had friends. Oh, Miss Millicent, may you never know such bitter trials! When I woke up my child was gone, and I never saw either Masterson or my boy again.'

'You waited in the village where he left you?' asked Millicent.

'For a year and over, Miss Milly, hopin' that he'd come back, bringing the boy with him; but no tidings ever came of him. At the end of that time I left word with the neighbors to say I was gone back to Compton, and I came straight here, when your father took me as his housekeeper, and where I lived happy for many years; but I've never forgotten my boy, Miss Millicent, and it's very seldom that I go to sleep without seeing his beautiful eyes shining upon me in my dreams.'

'Oh, Sally, Sally, how bitterly you have suffered, and what reason you have to hate this man's memory!'

'We've no call to talk harsh of them that's dead and gone, Miss Milly. Let 'em rest with their sins upon their own heads, and let us look to happier times. When Thomas Masterson went away, and left me without a sixpence to buy a loaf of bread, I never thought to be mistress of the Black Bear. Pecker has been a good friend to me, Miss, and a true, and I bless the Providence that sent him courting to the Hall—sitting of evenings in the housekeeper's room, never saying much, but always looking melancholic like, and dropping sudden on his knees one night, saying, "Sarah, will you have me?"'

Mr. Samuel Pecker here venturing to put his head into the room, and furthermore presuming to ask some question connected with the business of the establishment, was answered so sharply by his beloved wife that he retreated in confusion without obtaining what he wanted.

For the worthy Sarah, in common with many other wives, made a point of scrupulously concealing from her weaker helpmate any tender or grateful feeling that she might entertain for him; being possessed with an ever-present fear that if treated with ordinary civility he might, to use her own words, try to get the better of her.

So the dreary winter time set in, and, except for this honest-hearted Sally Pecker, and the pale curate's busy little wife, who had much ado to keep seven children fed and clothed upon sixty pounds a year, Millicent Duke was almost friendless. She was so gentle and retiring that she had never made many acquaintances. In the happy old time at the Hall, Darrell had been her friend, confidant and playfellow; and she had neither needed nor wished for any other. So now she shut herself up in her little cottage, with its quaint old mirrors and spindle-legged table; its grim arm-chairs of dark mahogany, and heavy oaken seats, that were too big to be moved by her feeble arms; she shut herself up in her prim, orderly little abode, and the Compton people seldom saw her except at Church, or on her way to the Black Bear.

Millicent heard nothing of Darrell directly, but he wrote about once in six weeks to Mrs. Sarah Pecker, who was sorely put to it to scrawl a few words in reply, telling him how Miss Millicent was but weakly, and how Captain Duke was still away with his ship, the *Vulture*. Through Sally, therefore, Mrs. Duke had tidings of this dear cousin. He had found friends in London, and had been taken as secretary to a noble Scottish lord, suspected of no very strong attachment to the Hanoverian cause; but it was not so long since other noble Scottish lords had paid the price of their loyalty, and there were ghastly and hideous warnings for those who went under Temple Bar; so whatever was done for the exiled family was done in secret—for the failures of the past had made the bravest men cautious.

CHAPTER VII.—How Darrell Markham Found his Horse.

While Millicent sat in the little oaken parlor at the Black Bear, with her head on Sarah Pecker's knee, and her melancholy blue eyes fixed upon the red recesses of the hollow fire, Darrell Markham rode westward through the dim November fog, charged with letters and messages from his patron, Lord C——, to some noble Somersetshire gentlemen, whose country seats lay very near Bristol.

On the first night of his journey, Darrell was to put up at Reading. It was dark when he entered the town, and rode between the two dim rows of flickering oil lamps straight to the door of the inn to which he had been recommended. The upper windows of the hostelry were brilliantly illuminated, and he could hear the jingling of glasses, and the noise of loud and riotous talk within. Though dark it was but early, and the lower part of the house was crowded with stalwart farmers, who had ridden over to the Reading market, and towns-people congregated about the bar to discuss the day's business.

Darrell flung the reins to the ostler, with a few particular directions about the treatment of his horse

'I will come round to the stable after I've dined,' Darrell said, 'and see how the animal looks; for he has a hard day's work before him to-morrow, and he must start in good condition.'

The ostler touched his hat, and led the horse away. It was a tall bony grey, not over handsome to look at, but strong enough to make light of the stiffest work.

They ushered Darrell up the broad staircase, and into a long corridor, in which he heard the same loud voices that had attracted his attention outside the inn.

'You have rather a riotous party,' he said to the landlord, who was carrying a pair of wax lights, and leading the way for his visitor.

'The gentlemen are merry, sir,' answered the man. 'They have been a long time over their wine. Sir Lovel Mortimer seems a rare one to keep the bottle moving amongst his friends.'

'Sir Lovel Mortimer?'

'Yes, sir.' A rich baronet from Devonshire, travelling to London with some of his friends.'

'Sir Lovel Mortimer,' said Darrell, thoughtfully; 'I know of no Devonshireman of that name.'

'He seems a gentleman used to great luxury,' answered the landlord; 'he has kept every servant in the house busy waiting upon him since he stopped here to dine.'

Darrell felt very little interest in the customs of this Devonshire baronet. He ate a simple dinner, washed down with half a bottle of claret, and then taking up a candle, went down stairs to ask the way to the stables.

The ostler came to him with a lantern, and leading him through a back door and across a yard, ushered him into a roomy, six-stalled stable. The stalls were all full, and as Darrell's grey horse was at the further extremity of the stable, he had to pick his way through wet straw and clover, past the other animals.

'Them there bay horses belongs to Sir Lovel Mortimer and his friends,' said the man; 'and very handsome beasts they be. Sir Lovel himself looks a pictur', mounted on this here bay.'

He slapped his hand upon the haunch of a horse as he spoke. The animal turned as he did so, and tossing up his head, looked at the two men.

'A tidy bit of horse-flesh, sir,' said the ostler; 'a hundred guineas' worth in any market, I should say.'

Darrell nodded, and striding up to the animal's head, threw one strong arm round its arched neck, and catching its ears with the other hand, dragged its face to a level with his own.

'I'd have you be careful, sir, how you handle him,' cried the ostler, with a tone of considerable alarm; 'the beast has a temper of his own; he tried to bite one of our boys not half an hour ago.'

'He won't bite me,' said Darrell, quietly. 'Give me the lantern here, will you.'

'You'd better let go of his head, sir; he's a stiffish temper,' remonstrated the ostler, drawing back.

'Give me the lantern, man; I know all about his temper.'

The ostler obeyed very unwillingly, and handed Darrell the lantern.

'I thought so,' said the young man, holding the glimmering light before the horse's face; 'and you knew your old master, Balmerino, eh, boy?'

The horse whinnied joyously, and snuffed at Darrell's coat-sleeve.

'The animal seems to know you, sir,' exclaimed the ostler.

'We know each other as well as ever brothers did,' said Darrell, stroking the horse's neck. 'I have ridden him for seven years and more, and I only lost him a 'twelvemonth ago. Do you know anything of this Sir Lovel Mortimer who owns him?'

'Not over much, sir, except that he's a fine high-spoken gentleman. He always uses our house when he's travelling between London and the west.'

'And is that often?' asked Darrell.

'Maybe six or eight times in a year,' answered the ostler.

'The gentleman is fonder of the road than I am,' muttered the young man 'Has he ever ridden this horse before to-day?'

The ostler hesitated, and scratched his head thoughtfully.

'I see a many bay horses, he answered, after a pause; 'I can't swear to this here animal; he may have been here before; but then, lookin' at it the other way, he mayn't.'

'Anyhow, you don't remember him?' said Darrell.

'Not to swear to,' repeated the man.

'I wouldn't mind giving a hundred pounds for this meeting of to-night, Balmerino, old friend,' murmured Darrell, 'though it was the last handful of guineas I had in the world!'

He returned to the house, and going up to the bar, called the landlord aside.

'I must speak to one of your guests up-stairs, my worthy host,' he said. 'Sir Lovel Mortimer must answer me two or three questions before I leave this house.'

The landlord looked alarmed at the very thought of an intrusion upon his important customer.

'Sir Lovel is not one to see over much company,' he said; 'but if you're a friend of his——'

'I never heard his name till to-night,' answered Darrell; 'but when a man rides another man's horse, he ought to be prepared to answer a few questions.'

'Sir Lovel Mortimer riding another man's horse!' cried the landlord, aghast. 'You must be mistaken, sir!'

'I have just left a horse in your stable that I could swear to as my own before any court in England.'

'A gentleman has often been mistaken in a horse,' muttered the landlord.

'Not after he has ridden him seven years,' answered Darrell. 'Be so good as to take my name to Sir Lovel, and tell him I should be glad of five minutes' conversation.'

The landlord obeyed very reluctantly. Sir Lovel was tired with his journey, and would take it ill being disturbed, he muttered; but as Darrell insisted, he went up-stairs with the young man's message, and returned presently to say that Sir Lovel would see the gentleman.

Darrell lost no time in following the landlord, who ushered him very ceremoniously into Sir Lovel's apartment. The room occupied by the west country baronet was a long wainscoted chamber, lighted by wax candles in sconces between the three windows and the panels in the opposite walls. It was used on grand occasions as a ballroom, and had all the stiff, old-fashioned grandeur of a State apartment. A pile of blazing logs sent the red flames roaring up the wide chimney, and in an easy chair before the open hearth lolled an effeminate-looking young man, in a brocade dressing-gown, silk stockings, with embroidered clocks, and shoes with red heels and glittering diamond buckles that emitted purple and rainbow sparks in the firelight. He wore a flaxen wig, curled and frizzed to such a degree that it stood away from his face, round which it formed a pale yellow frame, contrasting strongly with a pair of large, restless, black eyes, and the blue stubble upon his slender chin. He was quite alone, and in spite of the two empty punch bowls and the regiment of bottles upon the table before him, he seemed perfectly sober.

'Sit ye down, Mr. Markham,' he said, waving a hand as small as a woman's, and all of a glitter with diamonds and emeralds, 'sit ye down; and hark ye, Mr. William Byers, bring me another bottle of claret, and see that it's a little better than the last. My two worthy friends have staggered off to bed, Mr. Markham, a little the worse for this evening's bout, but you see I've contrived to keep my brains pretty clear of cobwebs, and am your humble servant to command.'

Sir Lovel Mortimer was as effeminate in manners as in person. He had a clear treble voice, and spoke in the languid, drawling manner of the maccaronis of Ranelagh and the Parks.

Darrell Markham told the story of his recognizing his horse in the stable below, in a few words.

'And you lost him——?' drawled Sir Lovel.

'A year ago last month.'

'Strange!' lisped the baronet. 'I gave fifty guineas for the animal at a fair at Barnstable last July.'

'Do you remember the person of whom you bought him?'

'Yes, perfectly. He was an elderly man, with white hair; he represented himself as a farmer from Dorsetshire.'

'Then the trace of the villian who robbed me is lost,' said Darrell. 'I would have given much had you got him straight from the scoundrel who robbed me of my purse and watch, and some documents of value to others besides myself, upon Compton Moor, last October.'

Sir Lovel Mortimer's restless black eyes flashed with an eager light as he looked at the speaker. Those ever restless eyes were strangely at variance with the young baronet's drawling treble voice and languid manner. It was as if the effeminate languor was only an assumption, the falsehood of which the eager, burning eyes betrayed in spite of himself.

'Will you tell me the story of your encounter with the knight of the road?' he asked.

Darrell gave him a brief description of his meeting with the highwayman, omitting all that bore any relation to either Millicent or Captain George Duke.

'I scarcely expect you to believe all this,' said Darrell, in conclusion, 'or to acknowledge my claims upon the horse; but if you like to come down to the stable, you will see at least that the faithful creature remembers his old master.'

'I have no need to go to the stable for confirmation of your words, Mr. Markham,' answered the young baronet; 'I would be the last to doubt the truth of a gentleman's assertion.'

The landlord brought the claret and a couple of clean glasses, while the two men were talking, and Sir Lovel pledged his visitor in a bumper.

The west country baronet seemed delighted to secure Darrell's society. He talked of the metropolis, boasted of his conquests among the fair sex, and slipping from one subject to another, began presently to speak of politics. Darrell, who had listened patiently to his silly prattle, grew grave immediately.

'You seem to take but little interest in either party, Mr. Markham,' Sir Lovel said at last, after vainly trying to discover the bent of Darrell's mind.

'Not over much,' answered the young man. 'I was bred in the country, where all we knew of politics was to set the bells ringing on the king's birthday, and pray for his majesty in church on Sundays and holidays.'

Sir Lovel shrugged his shoulders.

'What say you to our eating a broiled capon together?' he said. 'My friends were too far gone to hold out for supper, and I shall be very glad of your company over a bowl of punch.'

Darrell begged to be excused. He had to be on the road early the next morning, he said, and sadly wanted a good night's rest. The baronet would take no refusal; he rang the bell, summoned Mr. William Byers, the landlord, who waited his person upon his important guest, and ordered the capon and the punch.

'We can come to a friendly understanding about the horse while we sup, Mr. Markham,' said Sir Lovel.

Darrell bowed. The friendly understanding the two men came to was, that Markham would pay the baronet twenty guineas and give him the grey horse in exchange for Balmerino—the grey being worth about twenty pounds, and Sir Lovel being willing to lose ten by his bargain. So Darrell and the baronet parted excellent friends, and early the next morning Balmerino was brought round to the front door of the inn saddled and bridled for his old master.

The animal was in splendid condition, and, as Darrell sprang into the saddle, neighed proudly as he recognised the light hand of his familiar rider. The pavement of the Reading street clattered under his hoofs, and in ten minutes he was out upon the Bath road 'with the town melting into the distance behind him.

Darrell dined at Marlborough, and as the evening closed in with a thick white fog that shut him in on every side, he found himself in the loneliest part of the road between Marlborough and Bath. He had a well-filled purse, but he had a good pair of pistols, and felt safely armed against all attack. But, for the second time in his life, he had reason to repent of his rashness, for in the very loneliest turn of the road he heard the clattering of many hoofs close behind him, and by the time he had his pistols ready he was surrounded by three men, one of whom coming behind him threw up his arm as he was about to fire at the first of his assailants, while the third struck the same swinging blow upon his head that had laid him prostrate a year before upon the moorland road between Compton and Marley.

When Darrell Markham recovered his senses, he found himself lying on his back in a shallow, dry ditch; the fog had cleared away and the stars shone with a pale and chilly glimmer upon the winter landscape; the young man's pockets had been rifled and his pistols taken from him; but tied to the hedge above him stood the grey horse which he had left in the custody of the west country baronet.

Stupefied with the blow, and with every bone in his body stiff from lying for four or five hours in the cold and damp, Darrell was just able to get into the saddle and ride about a mile and a half to the nearest road-side inn.

The country people who kept this hostelry were almost frightened when they saw his white face and blood-stained forehead; but any story of outrage upon the high road found ready listeners and heartfelt sympathy.

The landlord stood open-mouthed as Darrell told of his adventure of the night before, and the exchange of the horses.

'Was the west country baronet a fine ladyfied little chap, with black eyes and small hands?' he asked eagerly.

'Yes.'

The man looked triumphantly round at the bystanders. 'I'm blest if I didn't think so,' he said. 'It's Captain Fanny.'

'Captain Fanny ?'

'Yes, one of the worst scoundrels in all the West of England, and the most difficult to catch. He's been christened Captain Fanny for his small hands and feet and his lackadaisical ways.'

The ostler came in as the landlord was speaking.

'I don't know whether you knew of this, sir,' he said, handing Darrell a slip of paper; 'I found it tied to the horse's bridle.'

The young man unfolded the paper and read these few words :—

'With Sir Lovel Mortimer's compliments to Mr. Markham, and in strict accordance with the old adage which says that exchange is no robbery.'

CHAPTER VIII.—How a Strange Pedlar worked a Great Change in the Mind and Manners of Sally Pecker.

Darrell Markham waited at the roadside inn till the tedious post of those days brought him a packet containing money from his friend and patron, Lord C——. He was vexed and humiliated at his encounter with Captain Fanny; for the second time in his life he had been worsted, and for the second time he found himself baulked of his revenge. The constable to whom he told the story of the robbery only shrugged his shoulders, and offered to tell him of a dozen more such adventures which had occurred within the last week or two; so Darrell had nothing to do but to submit quietly to the loss of his money and his horse, and ride on to execute his commissions in Somersetshire. Commissions from which little good ever came, as the reader knows; for it seemed as if that kingly house on which misfortune had so long set her seal was never more to be elevated from the degradation to which it had sunk.

All this time, while Darrell turned his horse's head from the west and journeyed by easy stages slowly back to town; while Sally Pecker at the Black Bear, and all Compton, from the curate, the lawyer, and the doctor, to the lowliest cottager in the village, was busy with preparations for the approaching Christmas; Millicent Duke waited and watched day after day for the return of her husband. All Compton might think the Captain dead, but not Millicent. She seemed possessed by some settled conviction that all the storms that ever rent the skies or shook the ocean would never cause the death of George Duke. She watched for his coming with a sick dread that every day might bring him. She rose in the morning with the thought that ere the early winter's night drew in, he would be seated by the hearth. She never heard a latch lifted, without trembling lest his hand should be upon it, nor listened to a manly foot-fall in the village high street without dreading lest she should recognize his familiar step. Her meeting with George Duke's shadow upon the moonlit pier at Marley had added a superstitious terror to her old dread and dislike of her husband. She thought of him now as a being possessed of unholy privileges. He might be near her, but unseen and impalpable; he might be hiding in the shadowy corners of the dark wainscot, or crouching in the snow outside the latticed window. He might be a spy upon her inmost thoughts, and knowing her distrust and aversion, might stay away for long years, only to torment her the more by returning when she had forgotten to expect him, and had even learned to be happy.

You see there is much to be allowed for her lonely life, her limited education, 'and the shade of superstition inseparable from a poetic temperament whose sole mental aliment had been such novels as people wrote and read a hundred years ago.

She never heard from her brother Ringwood, and the few reports of him that came to her from other sources only told of riot and dissipation, of tavern brawls and midnight squabbles in the streets above Covent Garden. She knew that he was wasting his substance amongst bad men, but she never once thought of her own interest in his fortune, or of the chances there might be of his death making her mistress of the stately old mansion in which she had been born.

Sally Pecker was in the full flood-tide of her Christmas preparations. Fat geese dangled from the hooks in the larder, with their long necks hanging within within a little distance of the ground; brave turkeys and big capons hung cheek by jowl with the weighty sirloin of beef which was to be the leading feature of the Christmas dinner. Everywhere, from the larder to the scullery, from the cellars to the sink, there were the tokens of plenty and the abundant promise of good cheer. In the kitchen, as in the pantry, Sally was the presiding deity. Betty, the cook-maid, plucked the geese, while her mistress made the Christmas pies and prepared the ingredients for the pudding, which was to be carried into the oak parlour on the ensuing day, garnished with holly and all a-blaze with burnt brandy. So important were these preparations, that as late as nine o'clock on the night of the twenty-fourth of December, found the maid and her mistress hard at work in the great kitchen at the Black Bear. This kitchen lay at the back of the house, and was divided from the principal rooms and the entrance-hall and bar by a long passage, which kept the clatter of plates and dishes, the smell of cooking, and all the other tokens of preparation, from the ears and noses of Mrs. Pecker's customers, who knew nothing of the dinner they had ordered, until they saw it smoking upon the table before them.

Sally Pecker and her maid were quite alone in the kitchen, for Samuel was busy with his duties in the bar, and the two chambermaids were waiting upon the visitors who had been dropped at the Bear by the Carlisle coach. The pleasant seasonable frost, in which all Compton had rejoiced, had broken up with that pertinacious spirit of contradiction with which a hard frost generally does break up just before Christmas, and a drizzling rain fell silently without the closely-barred window-shutters.

'I never see such weather,' said Mrs. Pecker, slamming the back door with an air of vexation after having taken a survey of the night; 'nothing but rain, rain, rain, coming down as straight as one of Samuel's pencil streaks between the figures in a score. Christmas scarcely seems Christmas in such weather as this. We might as well have ducks and green peas and cherry pie to-morrow, for all I can see, for it's so close and muggy that I can scarcely bear a good fire.'

The servants at the Black Bear knew the value of a good place and a peaceful life far too well ever to contradict their mistress, so Betty, the cook-maid, coincided immediately with Mrs. Pecker, and said that it certainly was hot—very much in the same spirit as that of the Danish courtier who was so eager to agree with Prince Hamlet.

The back door communicating with this kitchen at the Black Bear was the entrance generally used by any of the village tradesmen who brought Mrs. Pecker their goods, as well as by tramps and beggars and such idle ne'er do weels, who were generally sent off with a sharp answer from Sarah or her hand-maidens.

On this Christmas Eve Mrs. Pecker was expecting a parcel of groceries from the nearest market-town, which were to be brought to her by the Compton carrier.

'Purvis is late, Betty,' she said, as the clock struck nine, 'and I shall want the plums for my next batch of pies. Drat the man! he's gossiping and drinking at every house he calls at, I'll be bound.'

Betty murmured something about Christmas, and taking a friendly glass like, for the sake of the season; but Mrs. Pecker cut short her maid's apology for the delinquent carrier, and said sharply,

'Christmas or no Christmas, folks should attend to the business they live by; and as for friendly glasses, out of compliment to the season, it's a rare season that isn't a good season for drink with the men, for every wind that blows is an excuse for a fresh glass with them. I haven't kept the head inn in Compton without finding out what *they* are.'

It seemed as if the carrier had been aware of the contumely showered on his guilty head, for at this very moment a sharp rap at the window-shutters arrested Mrs. Pecker in the full torrent of her scorn.

'That's Purvis, I'll lay my life,' she exclaimed; 'the fool don't know the door from the window, because it's Christmas time, I suppose. Run, Betty, and fetch the parcel. You'll have to feel in my pocket for the sixpence, for I can't take my hands out of the flour.'

The girl hurried to open the door, and went out into the yard; but she presently returned to say that it wasn't Purvis, but a pedlar who wanted to show Mrs. Pecker some silks and laces.

'Silks and laces!' cried Sally; 'I want no such furbelows. Tell the man to go away directly. I won't have any such vagabonds prowling about the premises.'

The girl went back to the door, and remonstrated with the man, who said very little, and spoke in an indistinct, mumbling voice, that scarcely reached Mrs. Pecker's ears; but whatever he did say, it was to the effect that he would not leave the place until he had seen the mistress of the Black Bear.

Betsy came back to tell Mrs. Pecker this.

'Won't he?' exclaimed the redoubtable Sarah, raising her voice for the edification of the pedlar; 'we'll soon see about that. Tell him that we're not without constables in Compton, and that our magistrates are pretty hard against tramps and vagabonds.'

'But you won't be hard upon me, will you, Mrs. Pecker?' said the man, putting his head into the kitchen.

He was a stalwart, broad-shouldered fellow, with rather a Jewish nose, twinkling black eyes, and a complexion that had grown almost copper-coloured by exposure to all kinds of weather. He wore a three-cornered hat, which was trimmed with tarnished lace, and perched carelessly on one side of his head. His sleek hair was of a purplish black; and he wore a stiff black beard upon his fat double-chin. Gold ear-rings twinkled in his ears, and something very much like a diamond glittered amongst the dingy lace of his ragged shirt-frill. The bronzed, dirty hand with which he held open the box while he addressed Mrs. Pecker was bedizened by rings, which might have been either copper, or rich barbaric gold.

'You'll not refuse to look at the silks, Mrs. Sally,' he said, insinuatingly; 'or to give a poor tired chap a glass of something good on this merry Christmas night.'

Mrs. Pecker took her hands out of the flour; but white as they were, they were not a shade whiter than her usually rubicund face. For once in a way the landlady of the Black Bear seemed utterly at a loss for a sharp answer.

'You may come in,' she gasped, in a hoarse whisper, dropping into the nearest chair. 'Betty, go up-stairs, girl. I'll just hear what the man wants.'

But the cook was by no means inclined to lose the conversation between her mistress and the pedlar, whatever it might be; and accustomed as she was to obey, Mrs. Sarah Pecker, for once in a way she ventured to hesitate.

'If it's silk or laces, ma'am,' she said, 'I learnt a deal about 'em in my last place, for missus was always buyin' of Jews and pedlars: and I can tell you if they're worth what he asks for 'em.'

'You're very wise, my lass, I make no doubt,' answered the pedlar; 'but I daresay your mistress can choose a silk gown for herself, without the help of your advice. Get out of the kitchen, do you hear, girl?'

'Well, I'm sure,' exclaimed Betty, tossing her head, and not stirring from her post beside Mrs. Pecker.

'Do you hear, girl?' said the pedlar, savagely.—'Go!'

'Not for your tellin',' answered Betty· 'I don't like leavin' you alone with such as him, ma'am,' she said to her mistress. And then added in a whisper intended for Sally's ears alone, 'There's your silver watch hanging beside the chimney-piece, and three teaspoons on the dresser.'

'Go, Betty,' said Mrs. Pecker, in almost the same hoarse whisper with which she had spoken before. 'Go, girl, I shan't be above ten minutes choosin' a gown, and if the man wants to speak to me, he must have leave to speak.'

She rose with an effort from the chair into which she had fallen when the pedlar first put his head in at the kitchen door, and following Betty down the passage, saw her safely into the hall, and locked the door which separated the kitchen from the body of the house.

The pedlar was standing before the fire smoking a pipe when she returned to him after doing this. He had taken off his hat, and his long sleek black hair fell in greasy curls about his neck. He wore a claret-coloured coat, shabby and weather-stained, and high jack-boots, which smoked as he warmed his wet legs before the fire. 'Have you made all safe?' he asked, as Mrs. Pecker re-entered the kitchen.

'Yes.'

'No chance of listeners creeping about?—No eyes or ears at key-holes?'

'No.'

'That's comfortable. Now then, Sarah Pecker, listen to me.'

Whatever the pedlar had to say, or however long he was saying it, no one but the mistress of the Black Bear could have told. Betty, the cookmaid, with her eye and ear alternately applied to the keyhole of the door at the end of the passage, could only perceive, by the aid of the first organ, the faint glimmer of the firelight in the kitchen; while, by the help of the second, strain it how she might, she heard nothing but the gruff murmur of the pedlar's voice.

By-and-by that gruff murmur ceased altogether, and Betty began to think that the man had gone; but still Mrs. Pecker did not come to unlock the door and announce the departure of her visitor.

For upwards of a quarter of an hour Betty listened, growing every moment more puzzled by this strange silence.

'The man must have gone,' she thought; 'and missus has forgotten to call me back to the kitchen.'

She shook and rattled at the lock of the door.

'Please bring the key, ma'am,' she cried through the keyhole. 'The last batch of pies will be spoiled if they're not turned!'

Still no answer.

'Missus! missus!' she screamed at the top of her voice. Not a sound in reply to her appeal.

The girl still stood for a few minutes, with her heart beating loud and fast, wondering what this ominous silence could mean. Then a sudden terror seized her—she gave one sharp, shrill scream, and hurried off as fast as her legs would carry her, to look for Mr. Samuel Pecker.

Her fear was that this strange pedlar, with the barbarous rings in his ears, had spirited away the ponderous Sarah.

Samuel was seated in the wainscotted parlor, conversing with some of the Compton tradesmen, who were a little the worse for steaming punch and the influence of the season.

'Master! master!' cried the girl, thrusting her pale face in at the door, and troubling the festivity by her sudden and alarming appearance.

'What is it, Betty?' asked Samuel. Perhaps he, too, had taken some slight advantage of the season, and made himself merry, or, let us rather say, a shade less dismal than usual.

'Betty, what is it?' he repeated, drawing himself into an erect position, and looking defiantly at the girl, as much as to say,

'Who says I have been drinking?'

The cookmaid stood silently staring in at the door, and breathing hard.

'What is the matter, Betty?'

'Missus, sir.'

Something—surely it was not a ray of joy—some pale flicker of that feeble spirit lamp, which the parson of the parish told Samuel was his soul—illuminated the innkeeper's countenance as he said interrogatively,—

'Taken bad, Betty?'

'No, sir; but a pedlar, sir, a strange man, dark and fierce like, as asked to see missus, and was told to go about his business, for there was constables, but wouldn't, and offered missus silk gowns, and she turned me out of the kitchen—likewise locked the passage door—which, that's an hour ago and more, and —— please, sir, I think he must have run away with missus.'

Another ray, scarcely so feeble as the first, lit up the landlord's face as Betty gasped out the last of these semi-detached sentences.

'Your missus is rather heavy, Betty,' he murmured, thoughtfully; 'was the pedlar a big man?'

4

' He'd have made two of you, sir,' answered the girl.

' So he might, Betty; but two of me wouldn't be much agen Sarah.'

He seemed so very much inclined to sit down and discuss the matter philosophi-
cally, that the girl almost lost patience with him.

' The passage door is locked, sir, and I can't burst it open; hadn't we better
take a lantern and go round to the kitchen the other way ?'

Samuel nodded.

' You're right, Betty,' he said; ' get the lantern and I'll come round with you.
But if the man has run away with your missus, Betty,' he added, argumentatively,
' there's such a many roads and by-roads round Compton, that it wouldn't be over
much good going after them.'

Betty did not wait to consider this important point, but, lighting a bit of candle
in an old horn lantern, led the way into the yard.

They found Purvis, the carrier, standing at the back door.

' I've knocked nigh upon six times,' he said, ' and can't get no answer.'

Betty opened the door and ran into the kitchen, followed by Samuel and the
carrier.

The pedlar was gone, and stretched upon the hearth, in a dead swoon, lay Mrs.
Sarah Pecker.

They lifted her up, and dashed vinegar and cold water over her face and head.
There were some feathers lying at one end of the dresser, that Betty had plucked
from a fat goose only an hour or two before. Some of these, burned exactly under
Sarah's nostrils, brought her round.

' I'll lay a crown piece,' said Betty, ' that the watch and the silver spoons are
gone !'

Mrs. Pecker revived very slowly; but when at last she did open her eyes, and
saw the meek Samuel patiently awaiting her recovery, she burst into a sudden
flood of tears, and flinging her stout arms about his neck, indifferent to the
presence of either Betty or the carrier, cried out passionately—

' You've been a good husband to me, Samuel Pecker, and I haven't been an
indulgent wife to you; but folks are punished for their sins in this world as well
as the next, and I'll try and make you more comfortable for the future; for I
love you, my dear—indeed, I do !'

This unwonted show of emotion almost frightened Samuel. His weak blue
eyes opened to their widest extent in a watery stare, as he looked at his tearful
wife.

' Sarah,' he said, ' good gracious, don't ! I don't want you to be better to
me; I'm quite happy as we are. You may be a little sharp-spoken like now
and then, but I'm used to it now, Sally, and I should feel half lost with a wife
that didn't contradict me.'

' The spoons and the watch is gone,' exclaimed Betty, who had been inspecting
the premises; ' and missus's purse, I dare say. I knew that pedlar came here
with a bad meaning.'

' He did! he did!' cried Sarah Pecker.

It was thought a very strange thing by and bye in the village of Compton-on-
the-Moor that the mere fact of having been robbed of ten or twelve pounds worth
of property by a dishonest pedlar should have worked a reformation in the temper
and manners of Mrs. Sarah Pecker as regarded Samuel, her husband. But so it

was, nevertheless. Christmas passed away. Hard frosts succeeded drizzling rains, and drizzling rains melted hard frosts. Milder breezes, as the winter months fell back into the past, blew across Compton Moor; spring blossoms burst feebly forth in sheltered nooks beneath the black hedges, and the hedges themselves grew green in the fickle April weather, and still Sarah was mild of speech and pleasant of manner to her astonished husband.

The meek landlord of the Black Bear walked about as one in a strange but delicious dream. He had the key of his cellars, and was allowed to drink such portions of his own liquors as he thought fit; and Samuel did not abuse the unwonted privilege, for he was naturally a sober man. He was almost master in his own house. Sometimes this new state of things seemed well nigh too much for him. Once he went to his wife, and said to her, imploringly—

'Sarah, speak sharp to me, will you, please, for I feel as if I wasn't quite right in my head.'

CHAPTER IX.—SIR LOVEL MORTIMER'S DRUNKEN SERVANT.

I have said that Ringwood Markham was a milksop. In the days when men's swords were oftener out of the scabbard than in, the young squire had little chance of winning much respect in the gaming-houses and taverns that he loved to frequent, except by the expenditure of those golden guineas which his father had hoarded in the quiet, economical life the Markham family led at Compton Hall before the death of the old squire. The Hall property, which was by no means considerable, was so tightly tied up that Ringwood was powerless either to sell or mortgage it; and as he saw his father's savings melting away he felt that the time was not far distant when he must either go back to Compton, turn country gentleman and live upon his estate, or else sink to the position of a penniless adventurer hanging about the purlieus of the scenes in which he had once been all in all to half a dozen shabby toad-eaters, and the obsequious waiters of twenty different taverns.

Ringwood Markham had never been in love. He was one of those men who, secure from the tempest of passions that wreck sterner souls, sink in some pitiful quicksand of folly. With no shade of profligacy in his own lymphatic temperament, he was led by his vanity to ape the vices of the most profligate amongst his vicious companions. With an utter distaste to drinking, he had learned to become a drunkard; without any real passion for play, he had half ruined himself at the gaming-table; but, do what he would, he was still a girlish coxcomb, and men laughed at his pretty face, his silky golden hair, and small waist.

Darrell Markham and his cousin Ringwood had met once or twice in London, but the old quarrel was still rankling in the heart of at least one of the two men; and the coolness between them had never been abated. Darrell felt a contempt for Millicent's brother, which he took little pains to conceal; and it was only Ringwood's terror of his cousin that kept him from showing the hatred which had been engendered on the day of the one brief encounter between the two men. Darrell's sphere of action lay far away from the taverns and coffee-houses in which the young squire wasted his useless life. Too brave to drown his regrets in drunkenness or dissipation, he fought the battle of his own heart, and emerged a conqueror from the strife. True to the memory of the past, he was true also to the duties of the present. He had ambitious dreams that consoled him in those lonely hours in which his cousin Millicent's mournful face stole between him and the pages of some political pamphlet. He had high hopes for a future, which might be brilliant though it could never be happy; perhaps some dim foreshadowing of a day on which the good ship *Vulture* should go down under a tattered and crime-stained flag, and he and Millicent be left high and dry upon the shore of life.

In the summer succeeding that Christmas upon the eve of which the foreign-looking pedlar had robbed Mrs. Sally Pecker of three silver spoons, a Tompion watch, seven pounds twelve·shillings and four-pence in money, and her senses; while the mowers were busy about Compton in the warm June weather, Ringwood Markham was occupying a shabby lodging in the neighborhood of Bedford-street, Covent Garden. The young squire's purse was getting hourly lower; but though he had been obliged to leave his handsome lodgings and dismiss the man who had served him as valet for a couple of years, flattering his weaknesses, wearing his waistcoats, and appropriating casual handfuls of his loose silver; though he could no longer afford to spend a twenty-pound note upon a tavern supper, or shatter his wine-glass upon the wall behind him after proposing a toast, Ringwood Markham still contrived to wear a peach-blossom coat, with glittering silver lace, and to show his elegant person and pretty girlish face at his favorite haunts.

He spent half the day in bed, and rose an hour or two after noon, to lounge till dusk in a dirty satin dressing-gown, which was variegated as much with wine stains as with embroidered flowers, worked by Millicent's patient fingers years before. His dinner was brought from a neighboring tavern, together with a beer-stained copy of the *Flying Post*, in which Ringwood patiently spelt out the news, that he might be enabled to swagger and display his stale information to the companions of the evening. It was as he was poring over this very journal, with the June sunlight streaming into his shabby chamber, where the fine toilette of the evening lay side by side with the relics of the morning's breakfast, in the shape of an empty chocolate cup and the remains of a roll—it was during Ringwood's dinner-hour that he was disturbed by the slip-shod servant-maid of the lodging-house, who came to tell him that a gentleman, one calling himself Mr. Darrell Markham, was below and wished to speak with him.

Ringwood glanced instinctively to the space above the mantel-shelf, upon which there was a great display of pistols, rapiers, and other implements of warfare, and then, in rather a nervous tone of voice, told the servant girl to show the visitor up stairs.

Darrell's rapid step was heard upon the landing before the girl could leave the room.

'It is no time for ceremony, Ringwood,' he said, dashing into the apartment, ' nor for any old feeling of ill-will—I have come to talk to you about your sister.'

'About Millicent?'

Mr. Ringwood Markham's countenance evinced a powerful sense of relief as Darrell declared the object of his visit.

'Yes, about Mrs. George Duke. If your sister was dead and gone, Ringwood Markham, I doubt if you would have heard the news.'

'Millicent was always a poor correspondent,' pleaded the squire, who spent the best part of a day in scrawling a few ill-shaped characters and ill-spelt words over half a page of letter-paper; 'but what's wrong?'

'I scarce know if that which has happened may be well or ill for my poor cousin,' answered Darrell. 'Captain Duke has been away a year and a half, and no word of tidings of either him or his ship has reached Compton.'

Mr. Ringwood Markham opened his eyes and breathed hard by way of expressing strong emotion. He was so essentially selfish that he was a bad hypocrite. He had never learned to affect an interest in other people's affairs.

Darrell Markham was walking rapidly up and down the room, his spurs clattering upon the worm-eaten boards.

'I only got the news to-day,' he replied, 'in a letter from Sally Pecker. I had not heard from Compton for upwards of eight months, for it did me little good to have the old place brought to my mind; and to-day I got this letter from Sally, who says that the captain's return has long ceased to be looked for in Compton, except by Millicent, who still seems to expect him.'

'And what do you think of all this?' asked Ringwood.

'What do I think? Why, that Captain George Duke and his 'ship, the *Vulture*, have met the fate that all who sail under false colors deserve. I know those who can tell of a vessel with the word Vulture painted on her figure-head, that has been seen off the coast of Morocco, with the black flag flying at the fore, and a crew of Africans chained down in the hold. I know of those who can tell of a wicked traffic between the Moorish coast and the West India Islands, and who speak of places where the coming of George Duke is more dreaded than the yellow fever. Good Heavens! can it be that this man has met his fate, and that Millicent is free?'

'Free!'

'Yes, free to marry an honest man,' cried Darrell, his face flushing crimson with agitation.

Ringwood Markham had just intellect enough to be spiteful. He remembered the encounter in Farmer Morrison's kitchen, and said maliciously,

'Millicent will never be free till she hears certain news of her husband's death; if George Duke is such a roving customer as you make him out to be, his carcase may rot upon some foreign shore and she be none the wiser.'

'He has been away a year and a half,' answered Darrell; 'if he does not return within seven years from the time of his first sailing, Millicent may marry again.'

'Is that the law?'

'As I've heard it, from a boy. A year and a half gone; five years and a half to wait. My little Millicent, my poor Millicent, the time will be but a day, an hour, with such a star of hope to beckon me on to the end.'

Darrell sank into a chair against the open window, and buried his face in his hands.

Ringwood Markham could not resist the pleasure of inflicting another wound.

'I shouldn't wonder if the Captain is back before the summer is out,' he said; 'from what I know of George Duke, I think him no likely fellow to lose his life lightly, either on sea or land.'

Darrell took no notice of this speech. I doubt much if he even heard it. His thoughts had floated away on that one floodtide of hopeful emotion to the distant ocean of a happy future.

'Hark ye, Ringwood,' he said presently, rising and walking towards the door, 'I did not come here to talk lovers' talk. If George Duke does not return, Millicent will be a lonely and helpless woman for nearly six years to come, with nothing to live upon but the interest of the two thousand pounds the squire gave her on her marriage. I am but a poor man, but I claim a cousin's right to help her; but I must keep from her all knowledge of the quarter whence that help will come. You, as her brother, are bound to protect her. See that she wants for no comfort that can cheer her lonely life.'

If Ringwood had not been afraid of his stalwart cousin, he would have whimpered out some petty excuse about his own poverty; but as it was, he said, with rather a long face,

'I will do all I can, Darrell.'

Darrell shook hands with him for the first time since his quarrel, and left him to his toilette and his evening's dissipation.

Ringwood dressed himself in the peach-blossom and silver suit, and cocked his hat jauntily upon his flowing locks. In an age when periwigs were all the fashion, the young squire prided himself much upon the luxuriant natural curls which clustered about his high but narrow forehead. This particular evening he was especially careful of his toilette, for he had appointed to meet a gay party at Ranelagh, the chief of which was to be a certain west-country baronet, called Sir Lovel Mortimer, and better known in two or three taverns of rather doubtful reputation than in the houses of the aristocracy.

The west-country baronet outshone Ringwood Markham both in the elegance of his costume and the languid affectation of his manners. Titled ladies glanced approvingly at Sir Lovel's slim figure as he glided through the stately contortions of a minuet, and many a bright eye responded with a friendly scintillation to the flaming glances of the young baronet's great, restless black orbs. This extreme restlessness, which Darrell had perceived even in the apartment at the Reading inn, was of course a great deal more marked in a crowded assembly such as that in the brilliant dancing-room at Ranelagh.

The west-country baronet seemed ubiquitous. His white velvet coat, in which frosted rosebuds glittered in silk embroidery and tiny foil-stones; his diamond-hilted court sword and shoe buckles; his flaxen periwig, and burning black eyes flashed in every direction. His incessant moving from place to place rendered it almost impossible for any but the most acute observer to detect that Sir Lovel Mortimer had very few acquaintances among the aristocratic throng, and that the only persons whom he addressed familiarly were the four or five young men who had accompanied him, Ringwood Markham included.

The young squire was delighted at having made so distinguished an acquaintance. It was hard for the village-bred Cumbrian to detect the difference between the foil stones upon Sir Lovel's embroidered coat and the diamonds in his shoe-buckles; how impossible, then, for him to discover the wide varieties of tone in the west-country baronet's manners and those of the earls and marquises who lifted their eye-glasses to look at him. Ringwood followed Sir Lovel with a wide-open-eyed stare of respect and admiration, and when the place began to grow less crowded, and the baronet proposed adjourning to his lodgings in Cheyne Walk, and giving the party a broiled bone and a few throws of the dice, the squire was the first to assent to the proposition.

The young men walked to the baronet's house. It was not in Cheyne Walk, but an obscure street leading away from the river—a street in which the houses were small and gloomy.

Sir Lovel Mortimer stopped before a house, the windows of which were all dark, and knocked softly with his cane upon the panel of the door.

Ringwood, who had been already drinking a great deal, caught hold of the brazen knocker, and sounded a tremendous peal.

'You have no need to arouse the street, Mr Markham,' said the baronet, with some vexation; 'I make no doubt my servant is on the watch for us.

But it seemed as if Sir Lovel was mistaken, for the young men waited some time before the door was opened; and when at last the bolts were undone, and the party admitted into the house, they found themselves in darkness.

'Why, how's this, you lazy hound?' cried Sir Lovel, 'have you been asleep?'

'Yesh,' answered a thick, unsteady voice; 'sh'pose—I've been—'shleep.'

'Why, you're drunk, you rascal,' exclaimed the baronet; here, fetch a light, will you?'

'I'm feshin' a light,' the voice answered; 'I'm feelin' for tind' box.'

A scrambling of hands upon a shelf, the dropping of a flint and steel, and the rattling of candlesticks, succeeded this assertion; and in a few moments a light was struck, a wax candle lighted, and the speaker's face illuminated by a feeble flicker.

Sir Lovel Mortimer's servant was drunk; his face was dirty; his wig pushed over his eyebrows, and singed by the candle in his hand; his cravat was twisted awry, and hung about his neck like a halter; his eyes were dim and watery from the effect of strong liquors; and it was with difficulty he kept himself erect by swaying slowly to and fro as he stood staring vacantly at his master and his master's guests.

But it was not the mere drunkenness of the man's aspect which startled Ringwood Markham.

Sir Lovel Mortimer's servant was Captain George Duke.

About four o'clock the next afternoon, when Ringwood awoke from his prolonged drunken sleep, the first thing he did was to find a sheet of paper, scrawl half a dozen words upon it, fold it, and direct it thus :—

'Darrell Marnham, Esq.,
At the Earl of C——'s,
St. James's Square.'

The few words Ringwood scrawled were these :—

'Dear Darrell—George Duke is not ded. I saw him last nite at a hous in Chelsey. Yours to comand, R. MARKHAM.'

CHAPTER X.—THE HOUSE AT CHELSEA.

Darrell Markham had left London on some business for his patron when Ringwood's messenger delivered the brief lines telling of the young man's encounter with Captain George Duke.

It was a week before Darrell returned to St. James' square, where he found the young squire's letter waiting for him. One rapid glance at the contents of Ringwood's ill-spelled epistle was enough. He crumpled the letter into his pocket, threw his hat on his head, and without a moment's delay ran straight to the squire's lodging by Bedford street.

He found Ringwood lying in bed, spelling out the grease-stained pages of one of Mr. Fielding's novels. Tavern tankards and broken glasses were scattered on the table, empty bottles lay upon the ground, and the bones of a fowl and the remnants of a loaf of bread adorned the soiled table-cloth. Master Ringwood had entertained a couple of old friends to supper on the previous evening.

'Ringwood Markham,' said his cousin, holding out the young man's missive, 'what is the meaning of this?'

'Of which?' asked the squire, with a stupid stare. The fumes of the wine and ale of his last night's orgy had not quite cleared away from his intellect, somewhat obscure at the best of times.

'Of this letter, in which, as I think, you tell me the biggest lie that ever one man told another. George Duke in England—George Duke at Chelsea—what does it mean, man? speak!'

'Don't you be in a hurry,' said Ringwood, throwing his book into a corner of the room, propping himself up upon his pillow, and looking at Darrell with a species of half-tipsy gravity most ludicrous to behold; 'split me if you give a fellow time to collect his ideas. As to big lies, you'd better be careful how you use such expressions to a man of my reputation. Ask 'em round in Covent Garden whether I didn't offer to throw a spittoon at the sea captain who insulted me; and would have done it, too, if the bully hadn't knocked me down first. As to my letter, I'm prepared to stand to what I said in it. And now what did I say in it?'

'Look at it in your own hand,' answered Darrell, giving him the letter.

Ringwood spelt out his own epistle as carefully as if it had been some peculiar and mystic communication written in Greek or Hebrew; and then returning it to his cousin, said, with a toss of his pale golden locks that flung his silk night-cap rakishly askew on his forehead:

'As to that letter, Cousin Darrell Markham. the letter's nothing. What do you say to my finding George Duke, of the *Vulture*, acting as servant to my distinguished friend from Devonshire, Sir Lovel Mortimer, Baronet? What do you say to his taking Sir Lovel's orders, like any low knave that ever was? What do you say to his being in so drunken a state as to be sent away to bed with a sharp reprimand from his master, before I had the chance to speak a word to him?'

'What do I say to this?' cried Darrell, walking up and down the room in his agitation, 'why, that it can't be true. It's some stupid mistake of yours.'

'It can't be true, can't it? It's some stupid mistake of mine, is it? Upon my word, Mr. Darrell Markham, you're a very mannerly person to come into a gentleman's room and take advantage of his not having his sword at his side to tell him he's a fool and a liar. I tell you I saw George Duke, drunk, and acting as servant to my friend, Sir Lovel Mortimer.'

'Did George Duke recognize you?' asked Darrell.

'Don't I tell you that he was blind drunk!' cried the young squire, very much exasperated; 'how should he recognize me when he could scarcely see out of his eyes for drunkenness? I might have spoken to him, but before I could think whether 'twas best to speak or not, Sir Lovel had given him a kick and sent him about his business; and on second thoughts I reflected that it would be no great gain to expose family matters to the Baronet by letting him know that my brother-in-law was serving him as a lacquey.'

'But did you make no inquiries about this scoundrel?'

'I did. I told Sir Lovel I had a fancy that I knew the man's face, and asked who he was. The baronet knew nothing of him, except that he had served him for a twelve month, and was as faithful a fellow as ever breathed, though over-fond of drink.'

Darrell did not make any reply to his cousin's speech for some little time, but walked up and down the room absorbed in thought.

'Ringwood Markham,' he said at last, stopping short by the side of the bed, 'there's some mystery in all this that neither you nor I can penetrate. I know this Lovel Mortimer, the west-country baronet.'

'Then you know my very good friend,' said Ringwood, with a consequential smirk.

'I know one of the most audacious highwaymen that ever contrived to escape the Old Bailey.'

'A highwayman! The baronet—the mould of fashion and the glass of form—as lawless, the attorney, said of him; the most elegant beau that ever danced at Ranelagh; the owner of one of the finest estates in Devonshire. Have a care, Darrell, how you speak of my friends.'

'It would be better if you had more care in choosing them,' answered Darrell, quietly. 'My poor, foolish Ringwood, I hope you have not been letting this man clean out your pockets at hazard.'

'I have lost a few guineas to him at odd times,' muttered Ringwood, with a very long face.

The young squire had paid dearly enough for his love of fashionable company, and he had borne his losses without a murmur; but to find that he had been made a fool of all the while was a bitter blow to his self-conceit; still more bitter, since Darrell, of all others, was the person to undeceive him.

'You mean to tell me, then,' he said, ruefully, 'that this Sir Lovel——'

'Is no more Sir Lovel than you are,' answered Darrell; 'that all the fashion he can pretend to is that he has picked up on the king's highway; and that the only estate he will ever be master of in Devonshire or elsewhere will be enough stout timber to build him a gallows when his course comes to an abrupt termination. He is known to the knights of the road and the constables by the nickname of Captain Fanny, and there is little doubt the house in Chelsea to which he took you was a nest of highwaymen.'

Ringwood had not a word to say; he sat with his night-cap in his hand and one foot out of bed, staring helplessly at his cousin, and scratched his head dubiously.

'But that is not all,' continued Darrell, 'there is some mystery in the connexion between this man and George Duke. They might prove a dozen alibis, and they might swear me out of countenance, but prove what they may, and swear all they may, I can still declare that George Duke was the man who robbed me between Compton-on-the-Moor and Marley Water—George Duke was the man who stole my horse, and it was only seven months back that I found that very horse, stolen from me by that very George Duke, in the custody of this man, your friend, the baronet, alias Captain Fanny. The upshot of it is, that while we have thought George Duke was away upon the high seas, he has been hiding in London and going about the country robbing honest men. The ship *Vulture* is a fiction, and instead of being a merchant, a privateer, a pirate, or a slaver, George Duke is neither more nor less than a highwayman.'

'I only know that I saw him one night last week at a house in Chelsea,' muttered Ringwood, feebly. His weak intellect could scarcely keep pace with Darrell's excitement.

'Get up and dress yourself, Ringwood, while I run to the nearest magistrate; this fellow, Captain Fanny, stole my horse and emptied my pockets on the Bath road; we'll get a warrant out, take a couple of constables with us, and you shall lead the way to the house in which you saw George Duke; we'll unearth the scoundrels and find a clue to this mystery before night.'

'Two constables is not much,' murmured Ringwood, doubtfully. 'Sir Lovel always had his friends about him, and there may be a small regiment in that house.'

Darrell looked at his cousin with undisguised contempt.

'We don't want you to face the gang,' he said; 'we shall only ask you to show us the way and point out the house; you can run away and hide round the corner when you've done that, while I go in with the constables.'

'As to pointing out the house,' answered the crest-fallen squire, 'I'll give my help and welcome; but a man may be as brave as a lion, and yet not have any great fancy for being shot from behind a door.'

'I'll take the risks of any stray bullets, man,' cried Darrell, laughing; 'only get up and dress yourself without loss of time, while I go and fetch the constables.'

The getting of a warrant was rather a long business, and sorely tried Darrell's patience. It was dusk when the matter was accomplished, and the young man, returned to Ringwood's lodging with the two constables and the official document which was to secure the elegant person of Captain Fanny.

Darrell found his cousin specially equipped for the expedition, and armed to the teeth with a complicated collection of pistols, of the power to manage which he was as innocent as a baby. A formidable naval sword swung at his side, and got between his legs at every turn, while the muzzles of a tremendous pair of horse-pistols peeped out of his coat-pockets in such a manner that had they by any chance exploded, their charge must inevitably have been lodged in the elbows of the squire.

Darrell set his cousin's warlike toilette a little in order, Ringwood reluctantly consenting to be left with only one pair of pistols and a small rapier, in exchange for the tremendous cutlass he had placed so much faith in.

'It isn't the size of your weapon, but whether you're able to use it, that makes the difference, Ringwood,' said Darrell. 'Come along, my lad. We wont leave you in the thick of the fight, depend upon it.'

Ringwood looked anxiously into the faces of the two constables, as if to see whether there were any symptoms of a disposition to run away in either of their stolid countenances; and being apparently satisfied with the inspection, consented to step into a hackney-coach with his three companions.

Ringwood Markham was by no means the best of guides. The coachman who drove the party had rather a bad time of it. First, Ringwood was for going to

Chelsea through Tyburn turnpike, and could scarcely be persuaded that Ranelagh and Cheyne Walk did not lie somewhere in that direction. Then the young squire harassed and persecuted his unfortunate charioteer by suddenly commanding him to take abrupt turnings to the left, and to follow intricate windings to the right, and to keep scrupulously out of the high road that would have taken him straight to his direction. He grew fidgety the moment they passed Hyde Park corner, and was for driving direct to the marshes about Westminster, assuring his companions that it was necessary to pass the abbey in order to get to Chelsea, for he had passed it on the night in question; and at last, when Darrell fairly lost patience with him, and bade the coachman go his own way to Cheyne Walk without further waste of time, Millicent's brother threw himself back in a fit of the sulks, declaring that they had made a fool of him by bringing him as their guide, and then forbidding him to speak.

But when they reached Cheyne Walk, and leaving the coach against Don Saltero's tavern, set out on foot to find the house occupied by Captain Fanny, Ringwood Markham was of very little more use than before. In the first place, he had never known the name of the street; in the second place, he had gone to it from Ranelagh, and not from London, and that made all the difference in the finding of it, as he urged, when Darrell grew impatient at his stupidity; and then again, he had been with a merry party on that particular night, and had therefore taken little notice of the way. At last Darrell hit upon the plan of leading his cousin quietly through all the small streets at the back of Cheyne Walk, in hopes by that means of arriving at the desired end. Nor was he disappointed; for, after twenty false alarms, and just as he was beginning to give up the matter for a bad job, Ringwood suddenly came to a dead stop before the door of a substantial-looking house, and cried triumphantly,

'That's the knocker!'

But the young squire had given Darrell and the constables so much trouble for the last hour and a half by stopping every now and then, under the impression that he recognized a door-step, or a shutter, a lion's head in stone over the door-way, a brass bell-handle, a scraper, a peculiarly-shaped paving-stone, or some other object, and then, after a few moments deliberation, confessing himself to be mistaken, that, in spite of his triumphant tone, his cousin felt rather doubtful about the matter.

'You're sure it is the house, Ringwood?' he said.

'Sure! Don't I tell you I know the knocker? Am I likely to be mistaken, do you think?' asked the squire indignantly, quite forgetting that he had confessed himself mistaken about twenty times in the last hour. 'Don't I tell you that I know the knocker. I know it because I knocked upon it, and Sir Lov——he——the Captain, said I was a fool. It's a dragon's-head knocker in brass. I remember it well.'

'A dragon's head is a common enough pattern for a knocker,' said Darrell, rather hopelessly.

'Yes; but all dragon's heads are not beaten flat on one side, as this one is, are they?' cried Ringwood. 'I remember taking notice how the brass had been battered by some roysterer's sword-hilt or loaded cane. I tell you this is the house, cousin; and if you want to see George Duke, you'd better knock at the door. As I was a friend of Sir Lovel's, I'd rather not be seen in the matter; so I'll just step round the corner.'

With which expression of gentlemanly feeling, Mr. Ringwood Markham retired, leaving his cousin and the constables upon the door-step. It had long been dark, and the night was dull and moonless, with a heavy fog rising from the river.

Markham directed the two men to conceal themselves behind a projecting door-way a few paces down the street, while he knocked and reconnoitered the place.

His summons was answered by a servant girl, who carried a candle in her hand, and who told him that the west-country baronet, Sir Lovel Mortimer, had indeed occupied a part of the house, with his servant, and two or three of his friends, but that he had left three days before, and the lodgings were now to be let.

Did the girl know where Sir Lovel had gone ?' Darrell asked.

She believed he had gone back to Devonshire; but she would ask her missus, if the gentleman wished.

But the gentleman did not wish. He was so disappointed at the result of his expedition that he scarcely cared even to make an attempt at putting it to some trifling use.

But as he was turning to leave the door-step, he stopped to ask the girl one more question.

'This servant of Sir Lovell's,' he said, 'what sort of a person was he ?'

'A nasty, grumpy, disagreeable creature,' the girl answered.

'Did you know his name ?'

'His master always called him Jeremiah, sir; some of the other gentlemen called him sulky Jeremiah, because he was always grumbling and growling, except when he was tipsy.'

'Can you tell me what he was [like ?' asked Darrell. 'Was he a good looking fellow ?'

'Oh, as for that,' answered the servant girl, 'he was well enough to look at but too surly for the company of decent folks'

Darrell dropped a piece of silver into the girl's hand, and wished her good night. The constables emerged from their lurking-place as the young man left the door-step.

'Is it the right house, sir ?' asked one of them.

'Yes,' replied Darrell; 'we've found the nest sure enough, but the birds have flown. We must even make the best of it, my friends, and go home, for our warrant is but waste-paper to-night.'

They found Ringwood Markham waiting patiently enough round the corner He chuckled rather maliciously when he heard of his cousin's disappointment 'You'll believe me though, anyhow,' he said, 'since you found that it was the right house.'

'Yes, the right house,' answered Darrell, moodily; 'but there's little satisfaction in that. How do I know that this sulky servant of the highwayman's was really George Duke, and that you were not deceived by some fancied likeness ?'

CHAPTER XI.—AFTER SEVEN YEARS.

The star of the young squire, Ringwood Markham, shone for a very little longer in metropolitan hemispheres. His purse was empty, his credit exhausted, his health impaired, his spirits gone, and himself altogether so much the worse for his few brief years of London life, that there was nothing better for him to do than go quietly back to Compton-on-the-Moor, and take up his abode at the Hall, with an old woman as his housekeeper, and a couple of farm labourers for the rest of the establishment. This old woman had lived at Compton Hall while the shutters were closed before the principal windows, the heavy bolts fastened upon the chief doors, and the dust, cobwebs, and shadows brooding about the portraits of the dead and gone Markhams, whose poor painted images looked out with wan and ghastly simpers from the oaken wainscoting. The old housekeeper, I say, had led a very easy life in the dreary, darkened house, while Ringwood, its master, was roystering in the taverns about Covent Garden ; and she was by no means too well pleased when, in the dusk of a misty October evening, the young squire rode quietly up the deserted avenue, dismounted from his horse in the stable-yard, walked in at the back door leading into the servants' regions, and standing upon the broad hearth in the raftered kitchen, told her rather sulkily that he had come to live there.

His coming made very little change, however ; he established himself in the oak parlour, in which his father had smoked and drunk and sworn himself into his coffin ; and after giving strict orders that only the shutters of those rooms used by himself should be opened, he determinedly set his face against the outraged inhabitants of Compton. Now these simple people, not being aware that Ringwood Markham had spent every guinea that he had to spend, took great umbrage at his eccentric and solitary manner of living, and forthwith solved the enigma by setting him down a miser.

When in the dusk of the evening the squire crept out of the Hall gates, and strolling up to honest Sally Pecker's hospitable mansion, took his glass of punch in the best parlour of the inn, the Compton folks gathered round him and paid their homage to him as they had done to his father, when that obstinate-tempered and violent old gentleman was pleased to hold his court at the Bear. Ringwood felt that simple as the retired Cumbrian villagers were, they were wiser than the Londoners who had emptied his purse for him while they laughed in their sleeves at his dignity. Yes, on the whole, he was certainly happier at Compton than in his Bedford-street lodgings, or with his old tavern companions. He had been used to lead a very narrow life at the best, and the dull monotony of this new existence gave him no pain.

Millicent saw very little of her brother. He would sometimes drop into the cottage at dusk on his way to the Black Bear, and sit with her for a few minutes, talking of the village, or the farm, or some other of the every-day matters of life ; but his sister's simple society only wearied him, and after about a quarter of an hour he would begin to yawn drearily behind his hand, and then after kissing her upon the forehead as he bade her good night, he would stroll away to Sarah Pecker's, switching his light riding-whip as he walked, and pleased by the sensation his embroidered coat created among the village urchins and the idle women gossiping at their doors. It had been agreed between Darrell and Ringwood that Millicent was to know nothing of the house in Chelsea and the young squire's mysterious rencontre with George Duke or his shadow.

People in Compton—who knew of Darrell's encounter with the highwayman upon the moor, and of Mrs. Duke's meeting with the ghost upon Marley Pier—said that the Captain of the *Vulture* had his double, who appeared sometimes to those belonging to him, and whose appearance was no doubt a sign of trouble and calamity to George Duke. Such things had been before, they whispered, let the parson of the parish say what he would ; and there were some ghosts that all the Latin that worthy gentleman knew would never lay in the Red Sea.

The quiet years rolled slowly by unmarked by change, either at the Hall, the Black Bear, or the little cottage in which Millicent spent her tranquil days. No tidings came to Compton of the *Vulture* or its Captain, and though Millicent refused to wear a widow's dress, the feeling slowly crept upon her that she was indeed a widow, and that the tie knotted for her by others, and so bitter to bear, was broken by the mighty hand of death.

For the first year or two after Ringwood Markham's return, it was thought that he would most likely marry and take his place in the village as his father had done before him. The Hall estate was considered to be a very comfortable fortune in the neighborhood of Compton-on-the-Moor, and many a rich farmer's daughter sported her finest ribbons, and pinned her jauntily-trimmed hat coquettishly aslant upon her roll of glossy hair, in hopes of charming the young squire. But Ringwood's heart was a fortress by no means easy to be stormed : selfishness held her court therein, and complete indifference to all simple pleasures, and a certain weariness of life, had succeeded the young man's brief career of dissipation.

As his fortune mended with the first few years of his new and steady life, something of the miser's feeling took possession of his cold nature. He had spent his money upon ungrateful boon companions, who had laughed at him for his pains, and refused him a guinea when his purse was low. He would be warned by the past, and learn to be wiser in the future. Small tenants on the Compton Hall estate began to murmur to each other that Master Ringwood Markham was a hard landlord, and that times were even worse now for poor folks than in the old squire's day. These poor people spoke nothing but the truth. As Ringwood's empty purse filled once more, the young man felt a greedy eagerness to save money ; for what purpose he scarcely gave himself the trouble to think. Perhaps when he did think very seriously, a shuddering fear came over him that his impaired constitution was not to be easily mended—that even the fine north-country air sweeping across broad expanses of brown moorland, and floating in at the open windows of the oak parlour, could never bring a healthy glow back to his flushed cheeks ; and that it might be that he inherited with his mother's fair face something of her feebleness of constitution. But it was rarely that he suffered his mind to dwell upon these things. He was his own stewart, and rode a grey pony about the farm, watching the men at their work, and gloating over the progress of the crops as the changing seasons did their bounteous work, and the bright face of plenty met him in his way.

Northern harvests are late, and that harvest was especially late which was garnered in the seventh autumn succeeding the last sailing of the good ship *Vulture* from the harbor at Marley Water. September had been wet and cold, and October set in with a gloomy aspect, as of an unwelcome winter come before his due time. In the early days of this chill and cheerless October, they were still stacking the corn upon the Compton Hall farm, while Ringwood, on his white pony, rode from field to field to watch the progress of the men. The young squire was cautious and suspicious, and rarely thought that work was well done unless he was at the heels of those who did it.

He paid dearly enough for this want of faith in those who served him, for it was in one of these rides that he caught a chill that settled on his lungs, and threw him on a bed of sickness.

At the first hint of his illness, Millicent was by his side, patient and loving. eager to soothe and comfort, to tend and to restore. Like all creatures of his class, weak alike in physical and mental qualities, the young man peculiarly felt the helplessness of his state. He clung to his sister as if he had been a sick child and she his mother. In the dead of the night he would awake with the cold drops standing on his brow, and cry aloud to her to come to him; then, comforted and reassured at finding her watching by his side, he would fall into a peaceful slumber, with her hand clasped in his, and his fair head pillowed upon her shoulder.

The Compton doctor shook his head when he looked at the young squire's hectic cheeks and sounded his narrow chest. Not satisfied with the village surgeon's decision, Millicent sent to Marley Water for a physician to look at her sinking brother; but the physician only confirmed what his colleague had already said. There was no hope for Ringwood. Little matter whether they called it a violent cold, or a spasmodic cough, inflammation of the lungs, or low fever. All that need be told about him would have been better told in one word—consumption. His mother had died of it before him, fading quietly away as he was fading now.

In the dismal silence of those long winter nights in which the sick man awoke so often—always to see Millicent's fair face, lighted by the faint glimmer of the night-lamp, or the glow of the embers in the grate—Ringwood began to think of his past life—a brief life, which had been spent to no useful end whatsoever—a selfish life that had been passed in stolid indifference to the good of others—perhaps, from this terrible uselessness, almost a wicked life.

A few nights before that upon which the young squire died, he lay awake a long time counting the chiming of the quarters from the turret of Compton church, listening to the embers falling on the broad stone hearth, and the ivy leaves flapping and scraping at the window panes, with something like the sound of skeleton fingers tapping for admittance. And from this he fell to watching his sister's face as she sat in a low chair by the hearth, with her large, thoughtful blue eyes fixed upon the hollow fire, and the unread volume half dropping from her loose hand.

How pretty she was, he thought; but what a pensive beauty! How little of the light of joy had ever beamed from those melancholy eyes since the old days when Darrell and she were friends and playfellows, before Captain George Duke had ever shown his handsome face at the Hall. Thinking thus, it was only natural for him to remember his own share in forcing on this unhappy marriage; how he had persuaded his father to hear no girlish prayers, and to heed neither tears nor lamentations. Remembering this, he could but remember also the mean motive that had urged him to this course; the contemptible spite against his cousin Darrell, that had made him eager even for the shipwreck of his sister's happiness, so that her lover might suffer. He was dying now, and the world and all that was in it was of so little use to him, that he was ready enough to forgive his cousin all the old grudges between them, and to wish him well for the future.

'Millicent!' he said, by and bye.

'Yes, dear,' answered his sister, creeping to his side. 'I thought you were asleep. Have you been awake long, Ringwood?'

'Yes; a long time.'

'A long time! my poor boy.'

'Perhaps it's better to be awake sometimes,' murmured the sick man. 'I don't want to slip out of life in one long sleep. I've been thinking, Millicent.'

'Thinking, dear?'

'Yes; thinking what a bad brother I've been to you.'

'A bad brother, Ringwood. No, no, no!' She fell on her knees by the bedside as she spoke, and cast her loving arms about his wasted frame.

'Yes, Millicent, a bad brother. I helped to urge on your marriage with a man you hated. I helped to part you from the man you loved, and to make your young life miserable. You know that, and yet you're here, night after night, nursing me as tenderly as if I'd never thought but of your happiness.'

'The past is all forgiven long ago, dear Ringwood,' said his sister, earnestly; 'it would be ill for brother and sister if the love between them could not outlive old injuries, and be the brighter and the truer for old sorrows. I have outlived the memory of my misery long ago. Ringwood, dear, I have led a tranquil life for years past, and it seems as if it had pleased God to set me free from the ties that seemed so heavy to bear.'

'You will be almost a rich woman after my death, Milly,' said her brother, with a more cheerful tone. 'I have done a good deal in these last five years to improve the property, and you will find a bag full of guineas in the brass-handled bureau, where I keep all my papers and accounts. I think you may trust John Martin, the baliff, and Lawson and Thomas, and they will keep an eye upon the farm for your interest. You'll have to grow a woman of business when I'm gone, Milly, and it will be a fine change for you from yonder cottage in Compton High street to this big house.'

'Ringwood, Ringwood, don't speak of this!'

'But I must, Milly. It's time to speak of these things when a man feels he has not an hour upon this side of the grave that he can call his own. I want you to promise me something, Millicent, before I die; for a promise made to a dying man is always binding.'

'Ringwood dear, what is there I would not do for you?'

'I knew you wouldn't refuse. Now listen. How long has Captain Duke been away?'

She thought by this sudden mention of her husband's name that Ringwood's mind was wandering.

'Seven years, dear, next January.'

'I thought so. Now, Milly, listen to me. When the month of January is nearly out, I want you to take a journey to London, and carry a letter from me to Darrell Markham.'

'I'll do it, dear Ringwood, and would do more than that, if you wish. But why in January? Why not sooner?'

'Because it's a fancy I have; a sick man's fancy, perhaps. The letter is not written yet, but I'll write it before I fall asleep again. Get me the pen and ink, Milly.'

'To-morrow, dearest, not to-night,' she pleaded; 'you've been fatiguing yourself already with talking so much; write the letter to-morrow.'

'No, to-night,' he said, impatiently; "this very night, this very hour. I shall fall into a fever of anxiety if I don't write without a moment's delay. It is but a few lines.'

His loving nurse thought it better to comply with his wishes than to irritate him by a refusal. She brought paper, pens, ink, sealing-wax and seals, and a lighted candle, and arranged them on the little table by his bedside. She propped him up with pillows, so as to make his task as easy to him as possible, and then quietly withdrew to her seat by the hearth.

The reader knows how difficult penmanship was to Ringwood Markham even when in good health. It was a very hard task to him to-night. He labored long and painfully with the spluttering quill pen, and wrote but a few lines after all. These he read and re-read with evident satisfaction; and then folding the big sheet of foolscap very carefully, he sealed it with a great splash of red wax and the Markham arms, and addressed it in a feeble, sprawling hand, with many blots, to *Darrell Markham, Esq., to be delivered to him by Millicent Duke, at the close of January, 17—.*

'I have done Darrell many a wrong,' he said, as he handed the letter to his sister, 'but I think that this may repair all. It is my last will and testament, Milly. I shall make no other, for their is none to claim the property but you.'

'And you have left Darrell something then?' she asked.

'Nothing but that letter. I trust to you to deliver it faithfully, and I know that Darrell will be content.'

Mrs. Sarah Pecker came to the Hall whenever she had a spare moment, to help Millicent in her task of nursing the dying man. She was with her at that last dying moment, when the faint straws of life to which the young squire had clung floated one by one out of his feebled hands, and left him to be engulfed in Death's pitiless ocean.

CHAPTER XII.—CAPTAIN FANNY.

Six years had passed since that Christmas-eve upon which the foreign-looking pedlar robbed Mrs. Sarah Pecker, and worked such a wonderful change for the better in the fortunes and social status of her husband Samuel; and again Betty the cook-maid was busy plucking geese and turkeys; and again Mrs. Sarah stood at her ample dresser rolling out the paste for Christmas pies; again the mighty coal fire roared half-way up the chimney, and the capacious oven was like a furnace, and only to be approached with due precaution,—a glorious cavern out of which good things seemed for ever issuing;—big, sprawling, crusty, golden, brown-colored loaves, steaming batches of pies, small regiments of flat cakes of so little account as to be flung without ceremony upon the bare hearth, to grow cool at their leisure.

But for all that these Christmas preparations differed in no manner from those of a Christmas six years before, there were changes at the Bear—changes which the reader has already been told of. Mrs. Peeker had grown wondrously subdued in voice and manner. Something almost of timidity mingled with this new manner of the portly Sarah's—something of a perpetual uneasiness—a continual dread, no one knew of what. So changed, indeed, was she in this respect, that Samuel had sometimes to cheer her and console her when she was what he called "low," and to administer modest glasses of punch or comfortable hot suppers as restoratives.

While things were thus with Sarah, her worthy husband had very much improved under his better-half's new manner of treatment.

He was no longer afraid of his own customers nor of his own voice. He no longer trembled or blushed when suddenly addressed in conversation. He could venture to draw himself a mug of his own ale without looking nervously across his shoulder all the while. Samuel Peeker was a new man; still a little given to believe in ghosts, perhaps, and to be solemn when coffin-shaped cinders flew out of the fire; still a little doubtful as to going anywhere alone in the dark; but for all that a very lion of audacity and courage compared to what he had been before the foreign-looking pedlar threw Mrs. Peeker into a swoon.

The Bear was especially gay this Christmas-eve, for a party of gentlemen had ridden over from York, and were dining in the white parlor, a state apartment on the first-floor; they were to sleep that night and spend their Christmas-day at the inn, and the turkey lying helplessly in Betty's lap was set aside for them.

'And isn't one of 'em a handsome one, too?' said the cook, pulling vigorously at one of the biggest feathers. 'You should go in and have a look at 'un, missus—such black eyes, that pierce you through and through like a streak of lightning! and little white hands, just for all the world like Mrs. Duke's, and all covered with diamonds and such like. And ain't he a saucy one, too? and ain't the others afraid of him? The other two were for leaving here after dinner, and when he said he should stay, one of 'em asked if the place was——something, I couldn't catch the word; but he burst out laughing, and told him he was a lily-livered rascal, and not fit company for gentlemen, and the other rattled his glass on the table, and said the Captain was right—only he swore awful!' added Betty, with solemn horror.

While the cook was amusing her mistress with these details, Samuel put his head in at the kitchen door,

'Them bloods in the white parlour are rare noisy ones,' he said; 'they want half a dozen of the old port, and there's only three of them, and they've had Madeira and claret already. I wish you'd go up to 'em, Sarah, and give 'em a hint that they might be a little quieter. I'll go down for the wine, if you'll put yourself straight while I'm getting it.'

Sarah complied, wiped the flour from her hands, smoothed her cap-ribbons, and drew on her mittens by the time Samuel emerged from the cellar with two cobweb-shrouded black bottles under each arm.

'I've brought four, Sally,' he said, as he landed the precious burden on the kitchen table. 'I'll carry them up for you, and you can bring a few glasses.'

The trio in the white parlor was certainly rather ~~~~   air of massive wax candles burned in solid silver candle-sticks upon the polished oaken table, which was strewed with nuts, figs, raisins, oranges, and nut-crackers, and amply garnished with empty bottles and glittering diamond-cut wine-glasses. One of the party had flung himself back on his chair, and planted his spurred heels upon this very dessert table, while he amused himself by pealing an orange and throwing the rind at his opposite neighbor, who, more than half tipsy, sat with his elbows on the table and his chin in his hands, staring vacantly at his tormentor. The third member of the little party, and he who seemed far the most sober of the three, lounged with his back to the fire and his elbow leaning on the mantlepiece, and was in the midst of some anecdote he was telling as Mrs. Pecker entered the room. His flashing black eyes, and his small white teeth, which glittered as he spoke, lit up his face, which, in spite of his evident youth, was wan and haggard—the face of a man prematurely old from excitement and dissipation; the hand of time during the last six years had drawn many a wrinkle about the wrestless eyes and determined mouth of Sir Lovel Mortimer, Baronet, alias Captain Fanny, highwayman, and, on occasion, house-breaker. Heaven knows what there was in the appearance of either of the party to overawe or agitate the worthy mistress of the Black Bear, but certainly a faint and dusky pallor crept over Sarah Pecker's face as she set the wine and glasses upon the table. She seemed nervous and-uneasy under the strange dazzle of Captain Fanny's black eyes. I have said that they were not ordinary black eyes; indeed, there was something in them that the physiognomists of to-day would have set themselves industriously to work to define and explain. They were not only restless, but there was a look in them almost of terror—not of a terror of to-day or yesterday, but of some dim far-away time too remote for memory—some nervous shock received long before the mind had power to note its force, but which had left its lasting seal upon one feature of the face.

Sarah Pecker dropped and broke one of her best wine-glasses under the strange influence of these restless eyes. They fixed her gaze as if they had some magnetic power. She followed every motion of them earnestly, almost inquiringly, till the highwayman addressed her.

'We have the extreme honour of being waited upon by the landlady of the Bear in her own gracious person, have we not?' he said gallantly, admiring his small jewelled hand as he spoke. He was but a puny, almost wasted stripling, this dashing captain, and it was only the extreme vitality in himself that preserved him from insignificance.

Now at any other time Sarah Pecker would have dropped a curtsey, smoothed her muslin apron, and asked her guests whether their dinner had been to their liking; if their rooms were comfortable; the wine agreeable to their taste, and some other such hospitable questions; but to-night she seemed tongue-tied, as if the restless light in the Captain's eyes had almost magnetized her into silence.

'Yes,' she murmured, 'I am Sarah Pecker.'

'And a very comfortable and friendly creature you look, Mrs. Pecker,' answered Captain Fanny, with a sublime air of patronage. 'A recommendation in your own person to the hospitable shelter of the Bear; and, egad! Compton-on-the-Moor has need of some pleasant place of entertainment for the unlucky traveller who finds himself by mischance in its dreary neighborhood. Was there ever such a place, lads?' he added, turning to his two companions.

But Mrs. Sarah Pecker had been born in the village of Compton, and was by no means disposed to stand by and hear her native place so contemptuously spoken of. Turning her face a little away from the dashing knight of the road, as if it were easier to her to speak when out of the radius of those unquiet eyes, she said, with some dignity,

'Compton-on-the-Moor may be a retired place, gentlemen, being nigh upon a week's journey from London, but it is a pleasant village in summer time, and there are a great many noble families about.'

'Ah, by the bye,' replied Captain Fanny, 'we took notice of a big, red-brick, square-built house, standing amongst some fine timber, upon a bit of rising ground, half a mile on the other side of the village. A dull old dungeon enough it looked, with half the windows shut up. Who does that belong to?'

'It is called Compton Hall, sir,' answered Sarah, 'and it did belong to young Squire Ringwood Markham.'

'Ringwood Markham! A fair-faced lad, with blue eyes and a small waist?'

'The same, sir.'

'I knew him six years ago in London.'

'Very likely, sir. Poor Master Ringwood had his fling of London life, and very little he got by it, poor boy. He's gone now, sir. He was only buried three weeks ago.'

'And Compton Hall belonged to him?'

'Yes, sir; and Compton Hall farm, which brings in an income of four or five hundred a year.'

'And who does the Hall belong to now, then?' asked Captain Fanny.

'To his sister, sir, Miss Millicent that was—Mrs. Duke.'

'Mrs. Duke! The wife of a sailor—one George Duke?'

'The widow of Captain George Duke, sir.'

'The widow! What, is George Duke dead?'

'Little doubt of that, sir. The captain sailed from Marley Water seven years ago come January, and neither he nor his ship, the *Vulture*, have ever been heard of since.'

'And the widow of George Duke has come into a property worth four or five hundred a year?'

'Yes, sir; worth that, if it's worth a farthing.'

'And the only proof she has ever had of George Duke's death is his seven years' absence from Compton-on-the-Moor?'

'She could scarcely need a stronger proof, I should think, sir.'

'Couldn't she?' exclaimed the young man, with a laugh. 'Why, Mrs. Sarah Pecker, I have seen so much of the strange chances and changes of this world that I seldom believe a man is dead unless I see him put into his coffin, the lid screwed down upon him, and the earth shovelled into his grave; and even then there are some people such slippery customers that I should scarcely be surprised to meet them at the gate of the churchyard. The world is wide enough outside Compton-on-the-Moor: who knows that Captain Duke may not come back to-morrow to claim his wife and her fortune?'

'The Lord forbid!' said Mrs. Pecker, earnestly; 'I would rather not be wishing ill to any one; but sooner than poor Miss Millicent should see him come back to break her heart and waste her money, I would pray that the Captain of the *Vulture* may lie drowned and dead under the foreign seas.'

'A pious wish!' cried Captain Fanny, laughing. 'However, as I don't know the gentleman, Mrs. Pecker, I don't mind saying, Amen. But as to seven years' absence being proof enough to make a woman a widow, that's a common mistake, and a vulgar one, Mrs. Sarah, that I scarcely expected from a woman of your sense. Seven years—why, husbands have come back after seventeen!'

Mr. Pecker made no answer to this. If her face was paler even than it had been before, it was concealed from observation as she bent over the dessert-table collecting the dirty glasses upon her tray.

When she had left the room, and the three young men were once more alone, Captain Fanny burst into a peal of ringing laughter.

'Here's news!' he cried; 'split me, lads, here's a joke! George Duke dead and gone, and George Duke's widow with a fine estate and a farm that produces five hundred a year. If that fool, sulky Jeremiah, hadn't quarrelled with his best friends, and given us the slip in that cursed ungrateful manner, here would have been a chance for him!'

CHAPTER XIII.—THE END OF JANUARY.

Captain Fanny, otherwise Sir Lovel Mortimer, did not leave the Black Bear until the morning after Christmas day, when he and his two companions rode blithely off through the frosty December sunlight; after expressing much content with the festival fare provided by Mrs. Pecker; after paying the bill without so much as casting a glance at the items; after remembering the ostler, the chambermaid, the boots, and every other member of the comfortable establishment who had any claim to advance upon the generosity of the west-country baronet.

So entirely occupied were the domestics of the Black Bear in discussing their late distinguished visitor, that the news of a desperate highway robbery, accompanied by much violence, that had taken place near Carlisle, on the night of December the twenty-third, made scarcely any impression upon them. Nor were they even very seriously affected by an attack upon the York mail, the tidings of which reached them two days after the departure of Sir Lovel and his companions.

In the kitchen at the Black Bear, they spent the few remaining December evenings in talking of the gay young visitors who had lately enlivened the hostelry by their presence, while Millicent Duke, looking fairer and paler than ever in her mourning gown, sat alone in the oak parlour at Compton Hall, with the brass-handled bureau open before her, and her poor brains patiently at work, trying to understand some farming accounts rendered by her bailiff.

Mrs. George Duke found faithful Sarah Pecker an inestimable comfort to her in her bereavement and accession of fortune. I think, but for the help of that sturdy creature, poor Millicent would have made Compton Hall and Compton farm a present to the stalwart Cumbrian bailiff, and would have gone quietly back to her cottage in the High street, to wait for the coming of death, or Captain George Duke, or any other calamity which was the predestined close of her joyless life.

But Sarah Pecker was worth a dozen lawyers, and half-a-dozen stewards. She attended at the reading of the will, in which her own name was written down for 'fifty golden guineas and a mourning-ring, containing my hair, in remembrance of much love and kindness, to cost ten guineas, and no less.' She mastered all the bearings of that intricate document, and knew more of it after one reading than even the lawyer who had drawn it up. She talked to Millicent about quarters of wheat, and hay and turnips, till poor Mrs. Duke's brain reeled with vague admiration of Sarah's prodigious learning. The stalwart bailiff trembled before the mistress of the Black Bear, and went into long stammering explanations to account for a quarter of a truss of hay that had been twisted into bands, lest he should be suspected of dishonesty in the transaction.

When all was duly settled and adjusted, Millicent Duke found herself almost a rich woman. Rich enough, at any rate, to be considered a very wealthy person by the simple inhabitants of Compton-on-the-Moor, unless indeed, the long-missing husband, Captain George Duke of the good ship Vulture, should return to claim a share in his wife's newly-acquired fortune.

The thought that there was a remote possibility, a shadowy chance of this, would send a cold-chill to Millicent's heart, and seem almost to stop its beating.

If he should come home! If, after all these years of fearful watching and waiting, of trembling at the sound of every manly footstep, and shuddering at every voice—if, after all, now that she had completely given him up—now that she was rich, and might perhaps by-and-bye be happy—if, at this time of all others, the scourge of her young life should return and claim her once more as his to hold and to torture by the laws of God and man! A kind of distraction would take possession of her at the thought. She would deliver herself up to the horrible fancy until she could call up the image of the Captain of the Vulture, standing on the threshold of the door, with the wicked, vengeful light in his brown eyes, and the faint, far-off, breezy perfume of the ocean hovering about his chestnut hair. Then casting herself upon her knees, she would call upon Heaven to spare her from this terrible anguish—to strike her dead before that dreaded husband could return to claim her.

The diamond ear-ring, the fellow of which Captain Duke had taken from her on the night of their parting at Marley Water, had been religiously kept by her in a little red morocco-covered jewel-box. She was too simple and conscientious a creature to dream of disobeying her husband's commands. She looked sometimes at the solitary trinket; and seldom looked at it without praying that she might never see its fellow. She wished George Duke no harm. Her only wish was that they might never meet again. She would willingly have sold the Compton property, and have sent him every farthing yielded by its sale, had she known him to be living, so that he had but remained away from her.

Millicent was the only person in Compton who entertained any doubt of Capt. Duke's decease. The seven years which had elapsed since his departure—years of absence, unbroken by a single line from himself, or by one word of tidings from any accidental source—the common occurrence of wreck and disaster upon the seas, the suspicions entertained by many as to the Captain's unlawful mode of life, all pointed to one conclusion—he was dead. He had gone to the bottom of the sea with his own vessel, or had been hewn down by the cutlass of a Frenchman, or the scimitar of a Moorish pirate. The story of Millicent's meeting with her husband's shadow upon the pier at Marley Water only confirmed this belief in the death of George Duke.

Of course, Millicent told her faithful friend, Sarah Pecker, of the letter written by Ringwood a few nights before his death, and to be delivered by her to Darrell Markham.

The two women looked long and inquisitively at the folded sheet of foolscap, with its sprawling red seal, wondering what mysterious lines were written on the paper; but the wishes of Millicent's dead brother were sacred; and as the first half of January drew to a close, Mrs. Duke began to think of her formidable journey to London.

She had never been further away from home than on the occasion of a brief visit to the city of York, and the thought of finding her way to the great metropolis filled her with something almost approaching terror. I doubt if an Englishwoman of this present year of grace would think as much of a voyage to Calcutta as poor Millicent thought of this formidable southward journey; but her staunch friend Sarah was ready to stand by her in this, as well as in every other crisis of life.

'You don't suppose you're going to find Mr. Darrell Markham all by yourself, do you, Miss Millicent?' asked Sarah, when the business was discussed.

'Why, who should go with me, Sally dear?'

'Ah, who indeed?' answered Sarah, rather sarcastically; 'who but Sally Pecker, of the Black Bear, that nursed you when you was a baby; who else, I should like to know?'

'You, Sally?'

'Yes, me. I'd send Samuel with you, Miss Millicent, dear, for there's something respectable in the looks of a man, and we could put him into one of the old Markham liveries, and call him your servant; but Lord have mercy on us, what a lost baby that poor husband of mine would be in the city of London! I cannot send him to the market-town for a few groceries, without knowing before the time comes that he'll bring raisins instead of sugar, or have his pocket picked staring at some Merry Andrew. No, Miss Millicent, Samuel Pecker's the best of men; but you don't want a helpless infant to put you in the right way for finding Mr. Darrell; so you must take me with you, and make the best of a bad bargain.'

'My dear, good, kind, faithful Sally! But what will they do without you at the Bear? It will be near upon a fortnight's journey to London and back, allowing for some delay in the return coach; what will they do?'

'Why, do their best, Miss Millicent, to be sure; and a pretty muddle I shall find the place in when I come back, I dare say; but don't let the thought of that worry you, Miss Milly; I shan't mind it a bit. I sometimes fancy things go too smooth at the Bear, and I think the servants do their work well for sheer provocation.'

Sarah Pecker was so thoroughly determined upon accompanying Millicent, that Mrs. George Duke yielded with a good grace, thanked her stout protectress, and set to work to trim a mourning hat with ruches and streamers of black crape. It was Sarah who devised the trimmings for the coquettish little hat, and it was Sarah who found some jet ornaments amongst a chestful of clothes that had belonged to Millicent's mother, wherewith to adorn Mrs. Duke's fair neck and arms.

'There is no need for Mr. Darrell to find you changed for the worse in these seven years, Miss Milly, Sarah remarked, as she fastened the jet necklace rou her Millicent's slender throat. 'These black clothes are vastly becoming to your [?] skin : and I scarce think that our Darrell will be ashamed of his country cousi [?] for all the fine London madams he may have seen since he'left Compton.'   [?]

Mrs. Sarah Pecker had a natural and almost religious horror of the fair inha[?] tants of the metropolis, whom she dignified with the generic appellation of 'Lo[?] don madams.' She firmly believed the feminine portion of the population of tha[?] unknown city to be, without exception, frivolous, dissipated, faro-playing, masque-rade-haunting, painted, patched, and bedizened creatures, whose sole end and aim was to lure honest young country squires from legitimate attachments to rosy-cheeked kinswomen at home.

It was a cheerless and foggy morning that welcomed Millicent and her sturdy protectress to the great metropolis. Sarah Pecker, putting her head out of the coach window, at the village of Islington, saw a thick mass of blackness and cloud looming in a valley before her, and was told by a travelled passenger that it (the blackness and the cloud,) was London. It was at a ponderous, roomy inn, upon Snow-hill, that Millicent Duke and Sarah were deposited, with the one small trunk that formed all their luggage. Mrs. Pecker entered into conversation with the chambermaid, who brought the travellers some wretched combination of a great deal of crockery and a very little weak tea and blue-looking milk, face-tiously called breakfast. She took care to inform that domestic that the pale young lady in mourning, who, worn out by travelling all night, had fallen asleep upon a hard, moreen-covered, brass-nail-studded sofa, that looked as if it had been constructed out of coffin-lids—Sarah took care, I say, to casually inform this young person that her companion was one of the richest women in all Cumber-land, and might have travelled post all the way from Compton to Snow-hill, had she been pleased to spend her money. Mrs Pecker, who had at first rather in-clined towards the chambermaid, as a simple, plain-spoken young person, took of-fence at the cool way in which she received this information, and classed her forthwith amongst the 'London madams.'

'Cumbrian gentry count for little with you, I make no doubt,' Sarah remarked with ironical humility; 'but there are many in Cumberland who could buy up your fine town folks, and leave enough for themselves after they'd made the bar-gain.'

After having administered this dignified reproof to the chambermaid, who (no doubt penetrated and abashed) seemed in a great hurry to get out of the room. Sarah condescended to ask the way to St. James's square, which she expected was either round the corner, or across the street; somewhere in the neighborhood of the Fleet, or Hatton Garden.

She was told that a coach or a chair would take her to the desired locality, which was at the Court end of London, and much too far for her to walk, more especially as she was a stranger, and not likely to find her way thither.

Mrs. Pecker stared hard at the chambermaid, as if she would very much have liked to convict her in giving a false direction; but being unable to do so, sub-mitted to be advised, and ordered a coach to be ready in an hour.

The 'London madams' Mrs. Pecker saw from the coach window, as she and her fair charge were driven from Snow hill to St. James's, looked rather pinched and blue-nosed in the bitter January morning. The snow upon the pavement

him to fall at his feet and tell her story? Then a sudden panic seized her, and she flung herself upon the ground, grovelling there and tearing her pale. golden hair, crying out again and again that she was a guilty and a miserable creature.

Then, above even the thought of her sin, more horrible even than this consciousness of guilt, arose the black shadow of her future life—her future life, which was to be spent with him—with this hated and dreaded being, who now had a good excuse for the full exercise of his jealous spite against her, suppressed before, but never hidden. She tried to think of what her life would be, the light of Heaven blotted out, the angry hand of offended Providence stretched forth against her, and the cruel eyes of George Duke watching and gloating upon her anguish till she dropped into the grave, and went to meet the eternal punishment of her sins.

The thought of these things maddened her. She went to a bureau opposite the empty fire-place, and opened a drawer. She was in the room which had once been occupied by her dead father and mother, and she remembered that in this drawer there were some razors that had belonged to the old squire. She found the case containing them, and taking one of them in her hand, looked at the shining blade.

'Oh, no,' she cried, piteously; 'no, no, no, I cannot die with my sins unrepented of.'

In her terror of herself and eagerness to escape temptation, she was awkward in shutting the razor; so awkward, that before she could succeed in doing it, the blade slipped between the old fashioned handle and cut her across the inside of her hand. Not a dangerous cut, nor yet a very deep one, but deep enough to send the blood spattering over the razor blade and handle, the oak flooring, the open drawer of the bureau, and the skirt of Millicent's mourning dress.

She thrust the razor back into the case, and the case into the drawer, and binding up her hand with a cambric handkerchief, sat down again by the empty hearth.

'Oh, if Sally were here—my good, faithful Sally—what a comfort she would be to me,' said Mrs. Duke.

The stillness and loneliness of the house oppressed her. She opened the window and looked out at the snow-covered garden below. The feathery flakes still falling, always falling, thick and silently from the starless sky, shut out the world and closed about the old house like a vast white winding-sheet. The casement from which Millicent looked was at that angle of the house which was most remote from the garden room; but she could see at the further end of the terrace the reflection of the lighted bay-window red upon the snow.

The red reflection made a luminous patch upon the ground, peculiarly bright when contrasted with the surrounding darkness.

As Millicent looked at this illuminated spot, some dark object crossed it rapidly, blotting out the light for a moment.

It was such a night of wretchedness and mystery, that this circumstance, which at another time might have alarmed her, by suggesting some one's prowling about the lonely house, made no impression upon Mrs. Duke's bewildered mind. She closed the casement, and, returning to the fire-place, sat down again.

But the silence and solitude were utterly intolerable to her; she took the candle in her hand, opened her chamber door, went out upon the landing-place, and

7

listened. Listened, she knew not for what—listened, perhaps hoping, for some sound to break that intolerable stillness.

She could hear the ticking of the clock in the hall below. Beyond that, nothing. Not a sound, not a breath, not a murmur, not a whisper throughout the house.

Suddenly—to her dying day she never knew how the idea took possession of her—she thought that she would go straight to the garden room, awake George Duke, make him an offer of every guinea she had or was to have in the world, and entreat him to leave her and Compton forever.

She would appeal to his mercy—no, rather to his avarice and self-interest; she knew of old how little mercy she need expect from him. She turned into the long corridor leading to the other end of the house. The door of the garden room was shut, and her right hand being wounded, and muffled in a handkerchief, she was some time trying to turn the handle of the lock. The blood from the cut across her hand had oozed through the bandage, and left red smears upon the old-fashioned brass knob.

Millicent was perhaps rather more than two minutes trying to open the door.

All was still within the garden chamber. The firelight shone in fitful flashes upon the faded tapestry and the dim pictures on the walls. Millicent crept softly round to the side of the bed upon which Captain Duke had thrown himself. The sleeper lay with his face turned toward the fire, and his hand still resting on the butt-end of his pistol—exactly as he had lain an hour before when he fell asleep.

Millicent remembered how her brother Ringwood had lain in this very room, dead and tranquil, but three months before. Awe-stricken by the stillness, terrified by the remembrance of that which she had to say, Millicent paused between the foot of the bed and the fire-place, wondering how she should awake her husband.

The fire-light, changeful and capricious, now played upon the sleeper's ringlets, lying in golden brown tangles upon the pillow, now glanced upon the white fingers resting on the pistol, now flashed upon the tarnished girding of the bed posts, now glimmered on the ceiling, now lit up the wall; while Millicent's weary eyes followed the light as a traveller, astray on a dark night, follows a Will-o'-the-Wisp.

She followed the light wherever it pleased to lead her. From the golden ringlets on the pillow to the hand upon the pistol, from the gilded bed posts to the ceiling and the wall, lower and lower down the wall, to the oaken floor, beside the bed, and to a black pool which lay there, slowly saturating the time-blackened wood.

The black pool was blood—a pool that grew wider every second, fed by a stream that was silently pouring from a hideous gash across the throat of Captain George Duke, of the good ship *Vulture*.

With one long cry of horror Millicent Duke turned and fled.

Even in her blind, unreasoning terror, she remembered that it was easier to escape from that horrible house by the glass door leading to the garden than by the staircase and the hall. This half-glass door was in a recess, before which hung the tapestry curtains. Millicent dashed aside the drapery, opened the door, which was only fastened by one bolt, and rushed down the stone steps, across the garden, along the neglected pathways, and out on to the high road.

The snow was knee-deep as she tottered through it onward toward the village street. She never knew how she dragged her weary limbs over the painful distance; but she knew that the clocks were striking three when she knocked at the door of the Black Bear.

Samuel Pecker, scared by the events of the day, and yet more terrified by this unwonted knocking, opened the door a few inches wide, and, candle in hand, looked out of the aperture.

So had he opened that very door for the same visitor more than seven years ago, upon a certain autumn night, when Darrell Markham lay above stairs in the blue room, sick and delirious.

'Who is it?' he asked, shivering in every limb.

'It is I—Millicent. Let me in, let me in, for the love of God let me in!'

There was such terror in her voice as made the innkeeper forgetful of any alarm of his own. He gave way before this terrified women, as all men must yield to the might of such intense emotion, and opening the door wide, let her pass by him unquestioned.

The hall was all ablaze with light. Darrell Markham, Mrs. Pecker, and the servants had come down half-dressed, each carrying a lighted candle. The night had been one of agitation and excitement; none had slept well, and all had been aroused by the knocking.

No unearthly shadow, or double, or ghost newly arisen in the grave-clothes of the dead, could have struck more horror to these people's minds than did the figure of Millicent Duke, standing amidst them, with her pale, dishevelled hair, damp with the melted snow, her disordered garments trailing about her, wet and bloodstained, her eyes dilated with the same look of horrified astonishment with which she had looked upon the murdered man, and her wounded hand, from which the handkerchief had dropped, dyed red with hideous smears.

She stood amongst them for some moments, nether speaking to them nor looking at them, but with her eyes still fixed in that horror-stricken stare, and her wounded hand wandering about her forehead till her brow and hair were disfigured with the same red smears.

With his own face blanched to the ghastly hue of hers, Darrell Markham looked at his cousin, powerless to speak or question her. Sarah Pecker was the first to recover her presence of mind.

'Miss Milly,' she said, trying to take the distracted girl in her arms, 'what is it? What has happened? Tell me, dear.'

At the sound of this familiar voice, the fixed eyes turned towards the speaker, and Millicent Duke burst into a long, hysterical laugh.

'My God!' cried Darrell, 'that man has driven her mad!'

'Yes, mad,' answered Millicent, 'mad! Who can wonder? He is murdered. I saw it with my own eyes. His throat cut from ear to ear, and the red blood bubbling slowly from the wound to join that black pool upon the floor. Oh! Darrell, Sarah, have pity upon me, have pity upon me, and never let me enter that dreadful house again!'

She fell on her knees at their feet, and held up her clasped hands.

'Be calm, dear, be calm,' said Mrs. Pecker, trying to lift her from the ground. 'See, darling, you are with those who love you—with Master Darrell, and with your faithful old Sally, and with all friends about you. What is it, dear? Who is murdered?'

'George Duke.'

'The Captain murdered! But who could have done, it, Miss Milly? Who could have done such a dreadful deed?'

She shook her head piteously, but made no reply.

It was now for the first time that Darrell interfered. 'Take her up stairs,' he said to Mrs. Peeker, in an undertone. 'For God's sake take her away. Ask her no questions, but get her away from all these people, if you love her.'

Sarah obeyed; and between them, they carried Millicent to the room in which Darrell had been sleeping. A few embers still burned in the grate, and the bed was scarcely disturbed, for the young man had thrown himself dressed upon the outside of the counterpane. On this bed Sarah Peeker laid Millicent, while Darrell with his own hands re-lighted the fire.

On entering the room he had taken the precaution of locking the door, so that they were sure of being undisturbed; but they could hear the voices of the agitated servants and the inn-keeper, loud and confused below.

Mrs. Peeker occupied herself in taking off Millicent's wet shoes, and bathing her forehead with water and some reviving essence.

'Blood on her forehead!' she said, 'blood on her hand, blood on her clothes! Poor dear, poor dear! what can they have been doing to her?'

Darrell Markham laid his hand upon her shoulder, and the inn-keeper's wife could feel that the strong man trembled violently.

'Listen to me, Sarah,' he said; 'something horrible has happened at the Hall. Heaven only knows what, for this poor distracted girl can tell but little. I must go down with Samuel to see what is wrong. Remember this, that not a creature but yourself must come into this room while I am gone. You understand?'

'Yes, yes!'

'You will yourself keep watch over my unhappy cousin, and not allow another mortal to see her?'

'I will not, Master Darrell.'

'And you yourself will refrain from questioning her; and should she attempt to talk, check her as much as possible?'

'I will—I will, poor dear,' said Sarah, bending tenderly over the prostrate figure on the bed.

Darrell Markham lingered for a moment to look at his cousin. It was difficult to say whether she was conscious or not; her eyes were half open, but they had a lustreless, unseeing look, that bespoke no sense of that which passed before them. Her head lay back upon the pillow, her arms powerless at her sides, and she made no attempt to stir when Darrell turned away from the bed to leave the room.

'You will come back when you have found out—— ?'

'What has happened yonder? Yes, Sarah, I will.'

He went down stairs, and in the hall found one of the village constables, who lived near at hand, and who had been aroused by an officious ostler, anxious to distinguish himself in the emergency.

'Do you know anything of this business, Master Darrell?' asked this man.

'Nothing more than what these people about here can tell you,' answered Darrell. 'I was just going down to the Hall to see what had happened.'

'Then I'll go with your honour, if it's agreeable. Fetch a lantern, somebody.'

The appeal to 'somebody' being rather vague, everybody responded to it; and all the lanterns to be found in the establishment were speedily placed at the disposal of the constable.

That functionary selected one for himself, and handed another to Darrell.

'Now, then, Master Markham,' he said, 'the sooner we start the better.'

Neither of the two men spoke to each other on the way to the Hall, except once, when the constable again asked Darrell if he knew anything of this business, and Darrell again answered, as he had answered before, that he knew nothing of it whatever.

'We shall have difficulty enough to get in,' said Darrell, as they groped their way towards the terrace, 'for the only servant I saw in the house was a deaf old woman, and I doubt if Mrs. Duke aroused her.'

'Then Mrs. Duke ran straight out of the house when the deed was done, and came to the Black Bear?'

'I believe so.'

'Strange that she did not run to nearer neighbors for assistance. The Bear is upwards of a mile and a half from here, and there are houses within a quarter of a mile.'

Darrell made no reply.

'See yonder,' said the constable; 'we shall have no difficulty about getting in—there is a door open at the top of those steps.'

He pointed to the half glass door of the garden room, which Millicent had left ajar when she fled. The light streaming through the aperture threw a zigzag streak upon the snow-covered steps.

The snow still falling, for ever falling through that long night, blotted out all foot-prints almost as soon as they were made.

'Do you know in which room the murder was committed, Master Darrell?' asked the constable as they went up the steps.

'I know nothing but what you know yourself.'

The constable pushed open the half-glass door and the two men entered the room.

The candle, burned down to the socket of the quaint old silver candlestick, stood where Millicent had left it on a table near the window. The tapestry curtain, flung aside from the door as she had flung it in her terror, hung in a heap of heavy folds. The dark pool between the bed and the fire-place had widened and spread itself, but the hearth was cold and black, and the bed upon which George Duke had lain was empty.

It was empty. The pillow on which his head had rested was there, stained red with his blood. The butt-end of the pistol, on which his fingers had lain when he fell asleep was still visible beneath the pillow. Red, ragged stains and streaks of blood, and one long gory line which marked what way the stream had flowed towards the dark pool on the floor, disfigured the bed-clothes; but beyond this there was nothing.

'He must have got off the bed and dragged himself into another room,' said the constable, taking the candle from his lantern and sticking it into the candlestick left by Millicent; 'we must search the house, Mr. Markham.'

Before leaving the garden room, he bolted the half-glass door, and then, followed by Darrell, went out into the corridor.

They searched every room in the great, dreary house, but found no trace of

Captain George Duke, of the good ship *Vulture*. The sharp eyes of the constable took note of everything, and amongst other things of the half-open drawer in the bureau in the room which Millicent had last occupied. In this half-open drawer he found nothing but the case of razors, which he quietly put into his pocket.

'What do you want with those ?' Darrell asked.

'There's blood-stains upon one of them, Mr. Markham. They may be wanted when this business comes to be looked into.'

In one of the smaller rooms they came upon the old woman, Mrs. Meggis, snoring peacefully, happily ignorant of all that had passed, and as there seemed little good to be obtained from awakening her, they left her to her slumbers.

Throughout the house there was no sign of plunder nor of violence, save the pool of blood in the garden chamber above.

'Whoever has done this business,' said the constable, looking gravely about him, and pointing to the plate upon the sideboard, ' is no common burglar.'

'You mean——'

'I mean that it hasn't been done for gain. There's something more than plunder at the bottom of this.'

They went once more to the garden room, and the constable walked slowly round the chamber, looking at every thing in his way.

'What's come of the Captain's clothes, I wonder ?' he said, rubbing his chin, and staring thoughtfully at the bed.

It was noticeable that no vestige of clothing belonging to Captain George Duke was left in the apartment.

CHAPTER XIX.—AFTER THE MURDER.

The grey January morning dawned late and cold upon Compton-on-the-Moor. The snow still falling, ever falling through the night, had done strange work in the darkness. It had buried the old village, and left a new one in its stead. An indistinct heap of buildings with roof-tops and gable-ends so laden with snow, that the inhabitants of Compton scarcely knew the altered outlines of their own houses.

A murder had been done at Compton-on-the-Moor. At that simple Cumbrian village, whose annals until now had been unsustained with this, the foulest of crimes, a murder had been done in the silence of the long winter's night, beneath that white and shroud-like curtain of thick falling snow—a murder so wrapped in mystery, that the wisest in Compton were baffled in their attempts to understand its meaning.

With the winter dawn every creature in Compton knew of the deed that had been done. People scarcely knew how they heard of it, or who told them; but every lip was busy with conjecture, and every face was charged with solemn import, as who should say, ' I am the sole individual in the place who knows the real story, but I have my instructions from higher authorities, and I am dumb.'

The constable had taken up his abode at the Hall for the time being, and sat in the little oaken parlour in solemn state, holding conference now and again with the semi-officials in his employ, who were busy, according to the current belief of Compton, looking for the body.

Under this prevailing impression, the semi-officials had rather a hard time of it, as whenever they emerged from the Hall gates they were waylaid and seized upon by some anxious Comptonian, eager to know 'if they had found it.'

The anxiety about the missing body of the murdered man was the strongest point in the Compton interest. Busy volunteers made unauthorized search for it in every unlikely direction. In chimney-corners and cupboards of unoccupied houses, in out-buildings, pigsties, and stables; in far-away fields where they went waist deep in snow, and were in imminent peril of altogether disappearing in un-looked-for pit-falls; in the church-yard; nay, some of the most sanguine spirits went so far as to request being favored with the keys of the church itself, in order that they might look for Captain Duke in the vestry cupboard, where a skillful assassin might have hidden him behind the curate's surplice.

The constable had been at the Black Bear early that morning to ask for an in-terview with Mrs. George Duke, in order to hear her statement about the murder, but Sarah kept watch and ward over Millicent, and she and Darrell and the vil-lage surgeon all protested against the unhappy girl being questioned until she had in some way recovered from the mental shock which had prostrated her; so the constable was fain to withdraw, after whispering some directions to one of the semi-officials, who, red-nosed, blue-lipped, and shivering, hung about the Black Bear all that day.

Millicent was indeed in no state to be questioned. She lay in the same dull stupor into which she had fallen between three and four o'clock that morning. Sarah Pecker and Darrell Markham, watching her tenderly through the day, could not tell whether she was conscious of their presence. She never spoke, but sometimes tossed her head from side to side upon the pillow, moaning wearily. It was a cruel and a bitter day of trial to Darrell Markham. He never stirred from his place by the bedside, only looking up every now and then, when Sarah returned after leaving the room to ascertain what was going on down stairs, to ask anxiously if anything had been discovered about the murder—if they had found the assas-sin or the body

It was quite dark, when the constable, after locking the doors of the principal rooms in the old house, and putting the keys in his pockets, gave strict directions to Mrs. Meggis to admit no one, and to keep the place securely barricaded. By dint of considerable perseverance, he contrived to make the old woman under-stand him to this extent, and then nodding good-naturedly to her, left her for the night, happily ignorant of what had been so lately done beneath the roof that sheltered her.

From the Hall, Hugh Martin, the constable, walked straight to a mansion about half-a-mile distant, which was inhabited by a certain worthy gentleman and county magistrate, called Montague Bowers. A very different man to that magistrate before whom Darrell Markham charged Captain Duke with highway robbery seven years before.

In the private sitting-room, study, or *sanctum sanctorum* of this Mr. Bowers, Hugh Martin, the constable, made his report, detailing every particular of his day's work. 'I've done according as you agreed upon this morning, sir,' he said; 'I've waited out the day, and kept all dark, taking care to keep my eye upon 'em up yonder; but I can't see any way out of it but one, and I don't think we've any course but to do as we said then.'

Hugh Martin was closeted with the justice for a considerable time after this, and when he left the residence of Mr. Bowers, he hurried off at a brisk pace in the direction of the village and through the high street to the door of the Black Bear. In the wide open space before that hostelry, he came upon a man lounging in the bitter night, as if it had been some pleasant summer's evening, whose very atmosphere was a temptation to idleness. This man was no other than the red-nosed and blue-lipped semi-official, who had been lounging about the neighborhood of the inn all that day. He was a constable himself, but so inferior in position to the worthy Mr. Hugh Martin, that he was only looked upon as an assissant or satellite of that gentleman. Useful in a fray with poachers, to be knocked down with the butt-end of a gun before the real business of the encounter began; good enough to chase a refractory youngster who had thrown pebbles at the geese in the village-pond, or to convey an erratic donkey to safe-keeping in the pound, or to induct a drunken brawler in the stocks, but fit for nothing of a higher character.

'All right, Bob?' asked Mr. Hugh Martin of this gentleman.

'Quite right.'

'Anybody left the inn?'

'Why, Pecker himself has been in and out, up and down, and here and there, gabbling and chatting like an old magpie, but that's all, and he's safe enough in the bar now.'

'Nobody else has left the place?'

'Nobody.'

'That's all right Keep on the lookout down here, and if I open one of those windows overhead and whistle, you'll know you are wanted.'

The appearance of the constable created intense excitement amongst the loungers at the bar of the Black Bear. They gathered round him, so eager for information that between them they very nearly knocked him down.

What had he discovered? Who had done it? What had been the motive? Had he found the weapon? Had he found the body? Had he found the murderer?

Mr. Hugh Martin pushed all these eager questioners aside without any wonderful ceremony, and, walking straight to the bar, addressed Samuel Pecker.

'Mr. Markham is up-stairs, is he not?' he asked.

'He is in the blue room, poor dear gentleman.'

'With the lady—his cousin?'

'Yes.'

'Then I'll just step up-stairs, Pecker, for I've a few words to say to him about this business.'

The bystanders had gathered so close about Mr. Martin as to contrive to hear every syllable of this brief dialogue.

'He has found out all about it,' they said, when the constable went up-stairs, 'and he's gone to tell Mr. Markham—very proper, very right, of course.'

In the blue room Millicent Duke sat with her fair head resting on Sarah Pecker's ample shoulder, on a great roomy sofa drawn close up to the fire, against which stood a table, with a tea-tray and old dragon china cups and saucers. On the opposite side of the fire-place sat Darrell Markham, his eyes still fixed upon his cousin with the same look of anxious watchfulness that had marked his face all that day. Millicent had recognized them, and talked to them during the last half hour, and had told them the brief story of the night before. How she had gone to George Duke's chamber with the intention of making an appeal to his mercy, and how she had found him with his throat cut from ear to ear—dead !

Sarah had taken off Mrs. Duke's blood-stained dress, and wrapped her in some garments of her own, which hung about her slender figure in thick clumsy folds ; but the hideous stains had been removed from her hands and forehead, and there was nothing now about her to tell of the horrors through which she had passed. She had told them nothing of her wounded hand, and indeed had spoken incoherently at the best, for her fragile spirit had received a shock from which it was not easy for her to recover.

Still she was mending fast, Mrs. Pecker said ; and sitting with her head on Sarah's shoulder, in the light of the cheerful fire, with the comfortable array of teacups and the shining silver teapot on the table before her, it was almost diffi-cult to believe that four-and-twenty hours had not yet passed since she had fled from the roof that sheltered her murdered husband.

Mrs. Pecker was holding a teacup to Millicent's lips, imploring her to drink, when Darrell Markham started from his chair, and running to the door, listened to some sound without.

' What's that ?' he exclaimed.

It was the tramp of a man's footstep upon the stair, the footstep of Mr. Hugh Martin, the constable.

Darrell's face grew even paler than it had been all that day ; he drew back, holding his breath, terribly calm and white to look upon. The constable tapped at the door, and, without waiting for an answer, walked in.

Hugh Martin carried a certain official-looking document in his hand. Armed with this, he walked straight across the room to the sofa upon which Millicent sat.

' Mrs. Millicent Duke,' he said, ' in the King's name I arrest you for the wilful murder of your husband, George Duke.'

Darrell Markham flung himself between his cousin and the constable.

' Arrest her !' he cried ; ' arrest this weak girl, who was the first to bring the tidings of the murder !'

' Softly, Mr. Markham, softly, sir,' answered the constable, opening the nearest window, and whistling to the watcher beneath. I am sorry this business ever fell to my lot ; but I must do my duty. My warrant obliges me to arrest you as well as Mrs. Duke.'

CHAPTER XX.—COMMITTED FOR TRIAL.

Millicent and Darrell were taken to a dreary, dilapidated building called the lock-up, very rarely tenanted save by some wandering vagrant, who had been found guilty of the offence of having nothing to eat ; or some more troublesome delinquent, in the way of a poacher, who had been taken in the act of appropriating the hares and pheasants of a neighbouring preserve.

To this place Hugh Martin, the constable, and his assistant, Bob, conducted gentle and delicately-nurtured Mrs. George Duke; and the only one privilege which the entreaties of Darrell and Sarah Pecker could obtain for her was the constable's permission to Sally to stop all night in the cell with the female prisoner.

Darrell prayed Hugh Martin to take them straight to the house of Mr. Montague Bowers, that any examination which had to take place might take place that very night; but the constable shook his head gravely, and said, that Mr. Bowers had made up his mind to wait till morning.

Millicent, lying on a truckle bed beneath the window and listening to the passing footsteps, remembered how often she had gone by that dismal building, and how utterly unmindful she had been of those within. She shuddered as she looked at the ragged damp stains on the plaster walls, that made themselves into ugly faces in the uncertain flicker of a rush-light, remembering how many helpless creatures must have lain there through long winter nights like this, conjuring hideous faces from the same crooked lines and blotches, and counting the cobwebs hanging from the roof.

Mrs. Pecker, wrapped in a grey woollen cloak, sat on a wooden stool by the bedside, with her head wresting on Millicent's wretched straw pillow. She had completely worn herself out with protestations against the arrest, and was fain to keep silence from sheer exhaustion.

'Oh, Miss Milly, Miss Milly, said Sally, if I had only been with you last night,' she said; 'I had half a mind to come down to the Hall after Mr. Darrell left you; but I knew I was no favorite with Captain Duke, and I thought my coming might only make him angry against you.'

The last footfall died away upon the snow, the last dim light faded out in the village street, the long winter night, seeming almost eternal to the two women, wore itself out, and the cheerless daybreak showed a wan and ghastly face at the barred casements of Compton jail.

A little after eight, Hugh Martin, the constable, unbolted the door of the cell, and tapped against the rotten woodwork for permission to enter.

He found Millicent sitting on the edge of the truckle bed, dressed and ready to accompany him. Her cheeks and lips were bloodless, and her eyes, encircled by purple shadows, seemed to have grown larger since the night of the murder; but she was perfectly collected. The constable, moved with pity for her youth and gentle nature, had brought her a dish of warm tea; which she drank patiently and gratefully, though every drop seemed to choke her. She asked several questions about Darrell Markham, and told the constable that her cousin could have little difficulty in proving his innocence, as he had left the Hall long before the commission of the murder; but she said nothing whatever of herself, or of the injustice of the charge made against her.

A coach, hired from the Black Bear, carried the two prisoners to the magistrate's house; but Hugh Martin took good care that Darrell and his cousin were kept apart, the young man sitting on the box beside the coachman. The family was at breakfast when the little party arrived, and the prisoners heard the pleasant prattle of children's voices, as they were ushered through the Hall into the magistrate's study. A grim chamber this Hall of audience, lighted by two narrow windows looking out upon the stables, and furnished with stiff, high-backed oaken chairs, ponderous tables, and a solemn-faced clock, calculated to strike terror to the heart of a criminal.

Here Millicent and Darrell, with Hugh Martin the constable, and Sarah Pecker, waited for Mr. Montague Bowers, Justice of the Peace, to make his appearance.

Hanging about the Hall and gathered round the door of this chamber, were several people who had persuaded themselves into the idea that they knew something of the disappearance of Captain Duke, and were eager to serve the State by giving evidence to that effect. The ostler, who had aroused the constable; half a dozen men who had helped in the ineffectual search for the body; a woman who had assisted in conveying Mrs. Meggis, the deaf housekeeper, to the spot that morning, and many others equally unconnected with the case were amongst these. There was therefore a general sensation of disappointment and injury when Mr. Montague Bowers, coming away from his breakfast, selected Samuel Pecker from amongst this group of outsiders, and bidding the inn-keeper follow him, walked into the chamber of justice, and closed the door upon the rest.

'Now, Mr. Pecker,' said the Justice, seating himself at the oaken table, and dipping a pen into the ink, 'what have you to say about this business?'

Taken at a disadvantage thus, Samuel Pecker had very little indeed to say about it. He could only breathe hard, fidget nervously with his plaited ruffles (he had put on his Sunday clothes in honor of the occasion,) and stare at the Justice's clerk, who sat pen in hand, waiting to take down the inn-keeper's deposition.

'Come, Mr. Pecker,' said the Justice, 'what have you to state respecting the missing man?'

Samuel scratched his head vaguely, and looked appealingly at his wife, Sarah, who sat by the side of Mrs. Duke, weeping audibly.

'Meaning him as was murdered,' suggested Mr. Pecker.

'Meaning Captain George Duke,' replied the Justice

'Ah, but there it is,' exclaimed the bewildered Samuel, 'that's just where it is. Captain George Duke. Very good; but which of them? Him as asked me the way to Marley Water seven years ago on horseback last October? you remember, Master Darrell, for you was by at the time,' said the inn-keeper, addressing himself to one of the accused. 'Him as Miss Millicent saw on Marley Pier, by moonlight, when the clocks were striking twelve? Him as came to the Black Bear the day before yesterday at three o'clock in the afternoon; or him as drank and paid for a glass of brandy between eight and nine that night and left a horse in our stables, which has never been fetched away?'

The busy pen of the clerk, scratching after Mr. Samuel Pecker, seemed to keep up a kind of race with that gentleman as it jotted down his words, which already occupied half a page of foolscap.

Mr. Montague Bowers stared hopelessly at the witness.

'What is this?' he demanded, looking at Sarah and the two prisoners in his despair; 'what, in Heaven's name, does it all mean?'

Whereupon Mr. Samuel Pecker entered into a detailed account of all that had happened at Compton-on-the-Moor for the last seven years, not forgetting even the foreign-looking pedlar, who stole the spoons; and, indeed, throwing out a feeble suggestion that the itinerant might be in some way connected with the murder of Captain George Duke. When urged to come to the point, after rambling over nearly three sides of foolscap, he became so bewilderingly obscure that it was only by pumping at him, by brief and direct questions, that the Justice approached any nearer to the object of the examination.

'Now, suppose you tell me, Mr. Pecker, at what hour Captain Duke left your house on the night before last.'

'Between eight and nine.'

'Good, and you next saw him——?'

'Between nine and ten, when I went to the Hall with Miss Millicent and Mr. Darrell.'

'Did Mrs. Duke and her husband appear to be on friendly terms?'

To this question Samuel Pecker made a very discursive answer, setting out by protesting that nothing could have been more affectionate than the conduct of Millicent and the Captain; and then going on to declare that Mrs. Duke had fallen prostrate upon the snow, bewailing her bitter fortune, and her husband's return; and further relating how she had never addressed a word to him, except once, when she suddenly cried out, and asked him why he had come back to make her the most guilty and miserable of women.

Here the inn-keeper came to an abrupt finish, in no wise encouraged by the terrific appearance of his wife, Sarah, who sat shaking her head at him fiercely, from behind the shelter of her apron.

It took a long time thereforefore altogether, before the examination of Mr. Samuel Pecker was concluded, and that rather unmanageable witness pumped completely dry. Enough, however, had been elicited from the inn-keeper to establish Darrell Markham's innocence of the charge brought against him, inasmuch as he had quitted Compton Hall in the company of Samuel, leaving Captain Duke alive and well at ten o'clock. Between that hour and the time of George Duke's disappearance, Millicent and the deaf housekeeper had been alone with the missing man. Montague Bowers congratulated the young man upon his having come so safely out of the business, but Darrell neither heeded nor heard him. He stood close against the chair in which his cousin sat, watching that still and patient figure, that pale, resigned face, and thinking with anguish and terror that every word which tended to exonerate him, only threw a darker shadow of suspicion upon her.

Darrell Markham was the next witness examined. All was revealed in that cruel scrutiny. The marriage at St. Bride's church, Ringwood's letter, the return to Compton, the surprise of Captain Duke's reappearance, hard words that had been spoken between the two men, Millicent's despair, and shuddering horror of her husband, and then the long blank interval of many hours, at the end of which Mrs. George Duke came, white and distracted, to the Black Bear to tell of a murder that had been done.

All this the clerk's busy pen recorded, and to this Darrell Markham signed his name, in witness of its truth.

Hugh Martin, the constable, described the appearance of the house. The absence of any sign of pillage or violence, the unbroken fastenings of the heavy oaken door, the undisturbed plate on the side-board, and lastly, the bloodstained razor found by him in the bureau.

From Mrs. Meggis, the deaf housekeeper, very little information of any kind could be extorted.

Sarah Pecker was also examined, but she could tell nothing more than her

husband had told already, and she broke down so often in sobs and pitying ejac-
ulations about her old master's daughter that Mr. Bowers was glad to make the
examination as brief as possible.

All these people duly examined, their depositions read over to them, and signed
by them, there was nothing more to be done but to ask the accused, Millicent
Duke, what she had to say.

She told her awful story with a quiet coherence, that no one there assembled
had expected from her. She described her horror at the Captain's return, and
the distracted state of her mind, which had been nigh upon madness all that cruel
night. She stated, as nearly as was in her power, the time at which she bade
him good night, and retired to the chamber farthest from the garden room—the
chamber which had been her mother's She grew a little confused here, when
asked what she had done with herself between that time (a little after eleven
o'clock,) and the discovery of the murder. She said that she thought she must
have sat, perhaps for hours, thinking of her troubles, and half unconscious of the
lapse of time. She told how, by and bye, in a passionate outburst of despair, she
thought of her father's old razors lying in that very chamber, within reach of her
hands, and remembered how one deep gash in her throat might end all her sorrow
upon this earth. But the sight of the murderous steel, and the remembrance of
the sin of such a deed, had changed her purpose as suddenly as that purpose had
sprung up in her heart, and she thrust the razor away from her in a wild hurry of
terror and remorse. Then, with but little questioning and with quiet self-posses-
sion, she told how that other purpose, almost as desperate as the first, had succeeded it in her mind; and how she had determined to appeal to George Duke,
imploring of him to leave her, and to suffer her to drag out her days in peace.
How, eager to act upon this last hope, she had gone straight to his room, and there
had found him lying murdered on his bed. The Justice asked her if she had
gone close up to the bedside to convince herself that the Captain really was dead.
No, but she had seen the fearful gash across his throat; the blood streaming from
the open wound, and she knew that he was dead.

She spoke slowly, faltering a little sometimes, but never embarrassed, though
the clerks pen followed her every word as unrelentingly as if he had been a re-
cording angel writing the history of her sins. There had been a death-like silence
in the room while she told her story, broken only by the scratching of the clerk's
pen and the ticking of the solemn-faced clock.

'I will but ask you one more question, Mrs. Duke,' said Montague Bowers;
'and I beg you, for your own sake, to be careful how you answer it. Do you
know of any person likely to entertain a feeling of animosity against your husband?'

She might have replied that she knew nothing of her husband's habits, nor of
his companions. He might have had a dozen enemies whose names she had never
heard; but her simple and guileless mind was powerless to deal with the matter
thus, and she only answered the question in its plainest meaning.

'No; no one.'

'Think again, Mrs. Duke; this is a terrible business for you, and I would not
for the world hurry you Do you know of no one who had any motive for wishing your husband's death?'

'No one,' answered Millicent.

'Pardon me, Mr. Bowers,' interrupted Darrell, 'but my cousin forgets to tell you that the Captain of the *Vulture* was at the best a mysterious individual. He would never have been admitted into our family but for a whim of my poor uncle, who at the time of his daughter's marriage was scarcely account ible for his actions. No one in Compton knew who George Duke was, or where he came from, and no one but the late Squire believed him when he declared himself to be a Captain in his Majesty's navy. Six years ago I made it my business to ascertain the truth of the matter, and found that no such person as Captain George Duke had ever been heard of at the Admiralty. Whatever he was, nothing of his past life was known to either his wife or her relatives. My cousin Millicent is not therefore in a position to answer your question.'

'Can you answer it, Mr. Markham?'

'No more than Mrs. Duke.'

'I am sorry, said Mr. Bowers, gravely, 'very sorry; for under these circumstances my duty leaves me but one course. I shall be compelled to commit Millicent Duke to Carlisle jail for the murder of her husband.'

A woman's shriek vibrated through the chamber as these words were said, but it came from the lips of Sarah Pecker, and not from the accused. Calm as if she had been but a witness of the proceedings, Millicent comforted her old friend, imploring her not to give way to this passion of grief, for that Providence always sets such things right in due time.

But Sarah was not to be comforted so easily. 'No, Miss Millicent, no,' she said; 'Providence has suffered innocent people to be hung before this, and Heaven forgive us all for thinking so little about them; Heaven forgive us for thinking so little of the poor, guiltless creatures who have died a shameful death. O! Mr. Darrell,' exclaimed Sarah, with sudden energy, 'speak, speak, Mr. Darrell, dear; Samuel Pecker, speak and tell his worship that of all the innocent creatures in the world, my old master's daughter is the most innocent; that of all the tender and pitiful hearts God ever made, hers is the most pitiful. Tell him that from her birth until this day her hand was never raised to harm the lowliest thing that lives; how much less, then, against a fellow-creature's life. Tell him that too Mr. Darrell, and he cannot have the heart to send my innocent darling to a felon's jail.'

Darrell Markham turned his face to the wall and sobbed aloud; nor did any of those present see anything unmanly in the proceeding. Even the clerk was moved to compassion, and something very much like a tear dropped upon the closely written pages of evidence. But, whatever pity Mr. Montague Bowers might feel for the helpless girl sitting before him, in all quiet patience and resignation, he held to the course which he considered his duty, and made out the warrant which was to commit Millicent Duke to Carlisle prison, there to await the spring assizes.

Millicent started when they told her that she would leave Compton for Carlisle as soon as the only post-chaise in Compton, which of course belonged to the inn and posting-house kept by Samuel Pecker, could be prepared for her; but evinced no other surprise whatever. The written depositions were folded and locked in the justice's desk, the clerk retired, and the prisoner was left in the safe keeping of Hugh Martin and his fellow-constable, to await the coming of the post-chaise which was to carry her the first stage of her dismal journey. Darrell and Sarah remained with her to the last, only parting with her at the door of the chaise. The young man took her in his arms before he lifted her into the vehicle, and pressed his lips to her cold forehead.

open mouth, and a gruff voice asked her what she meant by making such a d——d fool of herself.

Betty took courage, and, drawing a long breath of relief, asked her visitant what his business was, and if he wasn't ashamed of himself for turning a poor girl's 'whole mask of blood.' Not deigning to enter into any discussion upon this remarkable physical operation, the stranger pushed the cook aside, and strode past her into the great kitchen, dimly lighted by the expiring fire and one guttering tallow candle.

Relieved from her first terror, Betty was now able to perceive that this was a taller and bigger man than George Duke, and that his figure bore no resemblance whatever to that of the murdered sailor.

He stood with his back to the hearth, slowly unwinding a great woolen shawl from his neck, when she followed him into the kitchen. This done, he threw off his hat, pushed his great hand through his short grizzled hair, and stared defiantly at the girl.

The stranger was the foreign-looking pedlar who had robbed Mrs. Pecker of her watch, purse, and silver spoons, in that very kitchen, six years before. Yes, he was the foreign-looking pedlar, but by no means the same prosperous individual he had appeared at that period. A gaunt, terrible, half-starved vagabond stood upon that hearth, where once had stood the smart and prosperous foreign pedlar.

Betty was preparing to begin scream number two, when he thrust his hand suddenly into his pocket, and taking thence a great clasped knife, exclaimed fiercely :

'As sure as I stand here, woman, if you lift your voice above a whisper, I'll put such a mark upon that throat of yours as will stop your noise forever. Sit you down there,' he said, pointing to the chair upon which Betty had dropped her work when she rose to open the door. 'Sit you down there, my lass, and answer the questions I've got to ask—or——' Betty dropped into the chair indicated as submissively as if she had been before Mr. Montague Bowers, Justice of the Peace, and quietly awaited his pleasure.

She felt that she had done her duty, and that she could do no more.

'Where's your missus, my lass ?' asked the pedlar.

'Ill a-bed.'

'And your master ?'

Betty described Samuel's whereabouts.

'So,' muttered the man, 'your missus is ill a-bed, and your master is in the white parlour drinking wine with a gentleman. 'What gentleman ?'

Betty was not particularly good at remembering names, but after considerable reflection she said that, if she recollected right, the gentleman was called Sir Lovel Summat.

The pedlar burst into a big laugh—a harsh and hungry kind of cachination, which seemed to come from a half-starved frame.

'Sir Lovel Summat,' he said ; 'it isn't Mortimer, is it ?'

'Yes, it is,' replied Betty.

The pedlar laughed again. 'Sir Lovel Mortimer, is it ? Well, that's strange ! Very strange, that of all nights out of the three hundred and sixty odd as go to a year, Sir Lovel should pick this night for being at Compton-on-the-Moor. Has he often been here before ?'

'Never but once; and that was last Christmas.'

'And he's here to-night. It's a strange world. I know Sir Lovel Mortimer; and Sir Lovel Mortimer knows me—intimately.' Betty looked rather incredulous at this assertion. 'Ah, you may stare, my lass!' muttered the pedlar; 'but it's Gospel truth for all that. I suppose this barrowknight of yours wears a fine gold-laced coat now, don't he?'

'It's silver lace,' the girl answered; 'and the handle of his sword shines like diamonds.'

The pedlar laughed and flung himself into a chair, which creaked beneath his weight, reduced as he was.

'Look you here, missus cook,' he said, 'talking's poor work on an empty stomach, and I haven't had a mouthful to put in mine since the break of this cold winter's day; so I'll trouble you for a bit of victuals and a drop of drink before we go on any further.' Seeing something like hesitation in the girl's face, he brought his hand heavily down on the table with a terrible oath.

'Fetch me what I want,' he roared; 'd'ye hear? Do you think there's anything in this house that I can't have for the asking?'

In her confusion and terror she brought a strange selection of food from the well-stocked pantry. He ate with such savage rapidity that the immense amount of food lasted a very short time, and then pushing the dish away from him with a satisfied grunt, he gasped fiercely the one word, 'Brandy.'

Betty shook her head. She explained to him that drink of any kind was impossible, as the bar was locked and the key in her master's possession.

'You're a nice, hospitable lot of people,' said the pedlar, rubbing his hand across his greasy mouth; 'and you know how to make folks comfortable that have come from foreign parts on purpose for the pleasure of seeing you. Now, look you here; it's double business that has brought me all the way from the county of Hampshire to Compton-on-the-Moor, and that business is first and foremost to see your missus; and secondly, to meet a friend as I parted company with above a fortnight back, and as promised to meet me here, but I expect I've got here before him. Now, that friend is a gentleman bred and born, and his name is Cap'en George Duke, of the *Vulture*.'

Betty, the cook, clasped her hands imploringly. 'Don't,' she cried, 'don't! This makes two this blessed night; for him as is up stairs said he came here by appointment with the murdered gentleman.'

'What murdered gentleman?' Betty told the story which had been so often told within the last five days. Told it in rather a gasping and unintelligible manner, but still with sufficient clearness to make the pedlar acquainted with the one great fact of the Captain's murder.

'His throat cut from ear to ear on the very same night as he came back,' said the man; 'that's an awkward business. He'd better have stopped where he was, I reckon. So there was no money took, nor plate, and his pretty young wife is in Carlisle jail for the murder—that's a queer story. I always thought George Duke had the devil's luck and his own too, but it seems that it failed him at last.'

Now, the reader may perhaps remember that, on hearing of the murder, Captain Fanny had made an observation to the effect that the murdered man had been an unlucky fellow from first to last, proving thereby how much the opinions of two people may differ upon a given subject.

'So Cap'en Duke is murdered—a bad look out for me!' muttered the pedlar; 'for I had a hold upon my gentleman as would have made his house mine, and his purse mine to the end of my days. I'd best see your missus, without losing any more time, my lass. Is her room anywhere nigh the parlour where your master and the barrownight's a sittin'?'

'No; missus's room is at the other end of the corridor.'

'Then go and tell her that him as come here six winters ago, and took the little present as she was kind enough to give him, has come back, and wants to see her without loss of time.' The girl shuddered, but obeyed, after one brief, distrusting glance round the kitchen. The man saw the glance and laughed.

There's no spoons about,' he said, 'as I can see, even if I had a mind to take 'em. Look sharp and tell your missus.'

Sarah Pecker lay awake, with a great bible open upon the table by her bed. She lifted her head from the pillow as Betty ran breathless into the room, for she saw from the girl's face that something had happened.

'Again!' she cried, when the cook had told her of the man waiting below: 'again! How cruel, how cruel, that *he* should come at such a time as this, when my mind is full of the thoughts of poor Miss Millicent, and when I've been praying night and day for something to happen to clear her dear name. It does seem hard.'

'There's many things in this life that seems hard,' said a voice close against the half-open door, as the gaunt pedlar strode unceremoniously into the room. 'Starvation's hard, and a long tramp through the snow with scarce a shoe to your foot is hard, and empty pockets is hard, and many things more as I could mention. You may go, young woman,' he added, addressing himself to Betty, and pointing to the door, 'you may go; and remember that what I've got to say is more interesting to your missus than to you, so you've no need to listen outside; but just keep a lookout, and give us warning if either your master or his guest leave the white parlour. You understand; so go.' Lest, after all, she should fail in comprehending him, he laid his rough hand upon that particular part of her anatomy commonly called the scruff of the neck, and put her outside the room. This done, he locked the door, walked across the chamber, and seated himself deliberately in an arm chair by the sick woman's bed.

'Well, Mistress Sally,' he said, staring about the room as he addressed Mrs. Pecker, as if looking for any article of value that might lurk here and there in the shadowy light, 'I suppose you scarcely looked to see me in such trim as this?' He held up his gaunt arm and shook the torn coat-sleeve and the wretched rags of a shirt, to draw her attention to the state of his garments.

'I scarcely looked to see you at all after these six years,' she said meekly.

'Oh, you didn't, Mistress Pecker, as I believe they call you hereabouts? No thanks to you for the compliment you paid my good sense. You thought that after happening to come by chance into this part of the country, and finding you living in clover in this place, with money put by in the bank, maybe, and silver plate, and the Lord knows what—you thought as I was such a precious fool, after seein' all this, as to take about fifteen pound worth of property, and go away contented, and stay away for six years. You thought all that, did you, my lady?'

'I thought,' she said falteringly, 'I thought you might be pitiful enough, knowing what I had suffered from you in years gone by, and seeing that it had pleased Providence to make me happy at last—I thought even your hard heart might have taken compassion upon me, and that you would have been content to take all I had to give, and to have gone quietly away forever.'

The pedlar looked at her with a fierce, scornful smile. He lifted his arm for the second time, and this time he pushed back the rags and showed his wasted flesh. 'Does this look as if I should have compassion on *you?*' he cried savagely; 'on *you*, wallowing here in comfort and luxury, with good food to eat, and good wine to drink, and fires to warm you, and clothes to wear, and money in your pocket? Why, if I was to sit here from now until daylight talking to you, I could never make you understand what I've passed through in the six infernal years since I last came to this place.'

'You've been away at sea?'

'Never you mind where I've been. I haven't been where men learn pitifulness, and compassion, and such fine sentiments as you've just been talking of. I've been where human beings are more dangerous to each other than savage beasts; where men use their knives oftener than their tongues; and where, if ever there was a bit of love or pity in a poor wretch's heart, it gets trampled out and changed to hate. That's where I've been.'

'And you've come here to me to ask for money,' said Sarah, looking shudderingly at the man's gloomy face.

'Yes.'

'How much will do?'

'A hundred pound.'

She shook her head despairingly. 'I haven't thirty,' she said; 'every farthing I have is in that box yonder on the chest of drawers with the brass handles. The key's in the pocket of the gown that's hanging on the bed-post. You can take what there is, and welcome; but I've no more.'

'But you can get more,' answered the man; 'you can ask Mr. Samuel Pecker.'

'No, no!'

'You won't ask him?'

'Not for one penny.'

'Then I will; I'll ask him fast enough, and I'll tell him—'

'Oh, Thomas, Thomas!' She raised her hands imploringly and clung about him, as if to stop him from uttering some dreaded word; but he flung her back upon the pillow. 'I'll tell him that I'm your lawful husband, Thomas Masterson, and that at one word from me you'll have to pack out of this house, and tramp wherever I please to take you.'

For a moment she lay back upon the pillow, her whole frame rent with a tempest of sobs. Then suddenly raising herself, she looked the man full in the face, and said deliberately, 'Tell him, then, Thomas Masterson! Tell him as you're my lawful husband as deceived and deluded me when I was a poor, ignorant girl—as beat and half-starved me—as took me away from friends and home. Tell him that you're my lawful husband, as took my one and only child away from me while I was asleep, and as stayed away for seventeen long years to come and claim me when I was a good man's happy wife. Tell him that you're Thomas Masterson, smuggler and thief. But let me tell you first that if you dare to come between him and me, I'll bring those up against you as will make you pay a dear price for your cruelty.'

'You've your old high spirit, Mrs. Sarah, he said; 'and even sickness hasn't taken it out of you. You won't ask Samuel Pecker for the money?'

'Not for one farthing.'

'Suppose you wanted the money for some whim of your own, do you think he'd refuse it to you?'

'I know he wouldn't.'

'Suppose I had a secret to sell, and wanted a hundred pounds for the price of it, would you raise the money?'

'A secret?'

'Yes. You spoke just now of your son, as you were so uncommon fond of. Suppose I could tell you where he is—within easy reach of you—would you give me a hundred pounds for the information?'

'I know you, Thomas Masterson,' she said; 'it's poor work to try and deceive me.'

'Look here,' answered the pedlar; 'you're uncommon suspicious to-night; but I know if you take your Bible oath you wont break it. Swear to me upon this book, that if I tell you where your son is, and bring him and you together, you'll let me have the hundred pounds within a week!'

He closed the Bible and placed it in her hands: she pressed her lips upon the cover of the volume.

'I swear,' she said, 'by this blessed book.'

'Very good. Your son is now sitting with Samuel Pecker in the parlour at the other end of the corridor. He calls himself Sir Lovel Mortimer; but his friends, companions, and the Bow-street runners call him Captain Fanny, and he is one of the most notorious highwaymen that ever played fast and loose with Jack Ketch.'

CHAPTER XXII.—Mother and Son.

Samuel Pecker and his guest, seated over their wine in the white parlour, between the hours of eleven and twelve, were startled by the violent ringing of the bell communicating with Sarah's bedchamber. Samuel was too good a husband not to recognize the vibration of that particular bell. Without stopping to apologize to his distinguished visitor, he hurried from the room and along the corridor to Sarah's chamber. The pedlar had left this apartment under the care of Betty, who had been ordered by Mrs. Pecker to find the gaunt-looking wanderer sleeping room in one of the garrets in the roof, or in some loft over the stable. Thomas Masterson declared himself little scrupulous as to where he slept, so that he had a mattress or a heap of straw to lie upon, and room to stretch his legs.

Sarah was alone, therefore, when the landlord entered the room in answer to the loud summons on the bell.

The invalid, seated up in bed, stared wildly at him as he showed his frightened face upon the threshold of the door.

'Samuel,' she said, clasping her hands upon her forehead, as if to steady the bewilderment of the brain within, 'have I been mad or dreaming? Who have you yonder in the white parlour?'

'The gentleman that came at Christmas, Sarah; the gentleman——'

'The eyes; the restless, restless black eyes, like my baby's,' cried Sarah, in a voice that was almost a shriek. 'I ought to have known him by his eyes. I ought to have known——'

'Sarah,' he said, 'Sarah, what is it?'

'The eyes,' she repeated; 'the eyes of the child you've heard me tell of; the child I lost long before I knew you, Samuel; the child whose cruel father was my first husband, Thomas Masterson.'

'But what of him to-night, Sarah?'

'Ay, what of him to-night,' she repeated, wildly, pushing the hair off her fore-head with both her feverish hands; 'what of him to-night? Who is there in the white parlour?'

'Sir Lovel Mortimer,' answered Samuel.

'Sir Lovel Mortimer, known to his friends, companions, and the Bow-street runners, as Captain Fanny,' said Sarah, slowly, repeating the words of Thomas Masterson; 'let me see him.'

'Let me see him,' she repeated.

'See him—Sir Lovel Mortimer—the west-country baronet?'

'The youth with the black eyes; the poor unhappy boy; the—let me see him, let me see him.'

Samuel shrugged his shoulders hopelessly. We know that he was a simple and faithful creature. If his sick wife had asked him to carry the moon to her bed-side, he would, no doubt, have made some feeble effort to gratify her. It was a small thing, then, to shuffle along the corridor and request the baronet to visit the invalid's chamber. Sir Lovel might, perhaps, be skilled in blood-letting and pharmacy, as some country gentlemen were in those days, and might be able to reduce this terrible fever and delirium.

Indeed, it seemed as if his presence had some soothing influence upon the sick woman, for Sarah quietly motioned him to a seat by her bedside, and then turn-ing with a white but tranquil face to Samuel Pecker, bade him leave the room.

Being left alone with the young highwayman, she lay perfectly still for some moments, looking earnestly at the handsome face dimly illuminated by the candle burning on the table near the bed. Captain Fanny had been too well accustomed to meet with adventures in the erratic course of his short life to be much affected by the fancy of a sick woman; he sat, therefore, very quietly, playing with his sword-hilt, and waiting Sarah's pleasure to speak.

But the invalid lay so long in silence, gazing, ah, Heaven knows with what vague maternal love and yearning, at the sharp profile of that young face, worn thin with many a midnight brawl and revel, that at last the restless gentleman fairly lost patience.

'I don't suppose you sent for me for the pleasure of staring at me, ma'am,' he said. 'I'm no ill-looking fellow, perhaps; but I'm not like the waxen images in Westminster Abbey, only good to be looked at. It's getting late, and I've had a weary day of it,' he added, with a yawn; 'have you nothing to say to me?'

'Much, much; so much that it's hard to tell how to begin.'

The young man shrugged his shoulders, and fell to staring at the showy rings upon his white hands.

'I have heard ill news to-night,' said Sarah, slowly; 'sorrowful news of an only child that I thought was dead and gone.'

Captain Fanny made no reply. He thought the speaker's wits were bewildered, and that it was best to let her have her say without making any attempt to question or contradict her. But the next words she uttered brought the blood to his face and set his heart (which was not that of a coward,) beating at a gallop.

'There has been one here to-night,' she said, ' who has told me who and what you are.'

'You know me, then ?'

'Yes; you are a highwayman, and they call you Captain Fanny.'

He clutched her wrist in his thin, nervous hand. 'You'll not peach upon me ?'

'Of all the creatures upon this wide earth,' she said, 'I should be the last to do that.'

'Not that it would so much matter,' he muttered, speaking not to Sarah, but to himself. ' A few months, maybe a few weeks, more or less. It wouldn't matter, if it wasn't for Jack Ketch.'

He put his fingers to his throat, and trifled nervously with his laced cravat, as if he already felt the coarse hands of the hangman, and the rope about his neck.

'Henry Masterson,' said the sick woman, 'tell me where and how your life has been spent.'

She called him by a name which he had not heard for seventeen years, and the faint hectic flush faded away from his hollow cheeks, leaving them as white as the coverlet upon Sarah's bed. ' You wonder that I know your name,' said Mrs. Pecker; 'but, oh, my boy, my boy, the wonder was that when I saw you this Christmas lately past, I did not guess the reason of my trouble at the sight of you. As if there could be but one reason for that trouble. As if there could be more than one face in all the world to set my heart beating as it beat that night. As if I could feel what I felt then at the sight of any face but one, and that the one that was a baby's face four-and-twenty years ago, and looked up at me out of my own baby's cradle.'

'What do you mean ?' he said; ' what do you mean ? I have heard my father say that I was born in Cumberland, and that he deserted my mother, carrying me away with him when I was but a child in arms. What is it you mean by this wild talk ?'

The Bible which Sarah had kissed a short time before, lay open on the table by the bedside. She stretched out her hand, and laying it upon the page, said solemnly—'I mean, Henry Masterson, that I was the wretched wife and mother whom that bad man deserted, and that you are my only child.'

The young man dropped his head upon the coverlet and sobbed aloud, his mother weeping over him and caressing him all the while.'

'My boy! my boy!' she cried, 'have they told me the truth ? Is it true—— ?'

'That I am a thief and a highwayman ? Yes, mother; and that I have never been honest since my babyhood, or lived with honest people since I can remember. My father cuffed me and beat me, and half-starved me and neglected me, and left me for days and days together in some wretched den, forgetting that such a creature as his son lived upon the earth; but he did not forget to teach me to steal, and I was quick to learn my lesson. I ran away from him when I was ten years old, and lived with gipsies and tramps and thieves and vagabonds and beggars, till I was cleverer at all their wicked businesses than those that were three times my age, and they made much of me and pampered me for my pretty looks and my cleverness, till I left them for a higher way of life, and fell in with a man who was my master first and my servant afterwards, but who, from first to last, was one to stifle every whisper of my conscience and every hope of ever being a better man. The history of my life would fill twenty volumes, mother, but you might read the moral of it in three lines. It's been a straight race for the gallows from beginning to end,'

He had lifted his head to say all this. The tears he had shed were already half-dried by the fever of his flushed cheeks, and his eyes glittered with a burning light.

'Tell me, my boy,' said Sarah, clinging about this new-found son, 'tell me, is there any danger—any danger *for your life?*'

He shook his head mournfully.

'I've never cared much how or when I risked it,' he answered. 'I've well-nigh thrown it away for a wager before this; but I feel to-night as if I shold like to keep it for your sake, mother.'

'And is there any danger?'

'Every danger, if they scent out my whereabouts just yet awhile. But if I can only cheat the gallows for two months longer, Master Jack Ketch will be cozened of his dues.'

'How, my darling?'

'Because a learned physician in London told me a couple of weeks ago, after sounding my chest and knocking me about till I was fairly out of patience, that my lungs are for the most part gone, and that I have not three months to live.

CHAPTER XXIII.—THE FINDING OF THE BODY.

The body of George Duke was found.

Nigh upon two months had passed since that January night upon which Millicent Duke rushed half distraught into the hall at the Black Bear to tell her horrible story; for nigh upon two months the unhappy lady had languished in Carlisle jail.

The Captain's body was found in a dismal pool behind the stables at Compton Hall. How the hiding-place had come to be overlooked in that general search which had been made immediately after the murder, no one was able to say. Every man who had assisted in that search declared emphatically that he had looked everywhere; and yet it seemed clear enough that no one had looked here; for, as the end of March drew nigh, and the inhabitants of Compton were busy talking of Mrs. Duke's approaching trial, the draught-horses on the Compton Hall farm refused to drink the stagnant water of this pool, and a vile miasma rising from its shallow bosom set the slow brains of the farm-laborers at work to discover the cause of the mischief. A dismal horror was brought to the light of day by this search. The body of a man, rotted out of all semblance to humanity, was found lying at the bottom of that stagnant pool, as it had doubtless lain since that night in January, when the falling snow blotted away the traces of the murderer's feet, and fell like a sheltering curtain upon the footsteps of crime.

The stable-yard lay behind the prim flower-beds and straight walks of the little pleasure ground below the garden chamber in which George Duke had been murdered. Between the stable-yard and this neglected flower-garden there was no barrier but a quick-set hedge and a little wicket gate. From this gate to the pond behind the stables the distance was about thirty yards.

It was a likely enough place, therefore, for the murderer to choose for the concealment of his victim; but whoever had dragged the body of George Duke from the garden-chamber to this pool must have had another task to perform before his hideous work was done. Every piece of water in Compton had been frozen over on that January night; the murderer must, therefore, have broken a hole in the ice before throwing the body into the pond, and this hole being frozen over the next morning by daybreak, and the pond, moreover, being thickly covered with a bed of snow, it was scarcely so strange that those who searched for the body should have overlooked this hiding-place.

At the bottom of the pool was found the instrument which the murderer had doubtless used to break up the ice. It was a thick oaken walking-stick, the centre of which was hollowed out so as to conceal a rapier. The old squire had had a strange fancy for quaint walking-sticks, loaded canes, sword-sticks, and such weapons; and there could be little doubt that this oaken stick was taken from a collection of these things which had lain for years in a closet beside the parlor chimney.

The remains were carried into one of the empty chambers in Compton Hall, and a coroner's inquest was there held upon them.

No one seemed for an instant to entertain a doubt that this was the body of George Duke, although there was little enough about these decomposed remains by which to prove identity. The few rotting rags of clothing still hanging about the corpse consisted only of the shreds of a shirt, breeches and stockings. There was no trace of the shabby coat with the naval buttons, the three-cornered hat, waistcoat and boots, which the Captain wore on returning to Compton. Yet these things had disappeared on the night of the murder.

The coroner's jury took no pains to unravel this branch of the dismal mystery, and pronounced a verdict to the effect that a body—supposed to be the missing body of George Duke—had been found in a pond on the premises belonging to Compton Hall.

Millicent, in her cell at Carlisle, received the news of the discovery of the body, and the verdict which had followed that discovery, as calmly as if neither the one nor the other were to have any influence on her fate. The frail, womanly nature had been so shaken by the horrors of that January night, that even the thought of a shameful death could scarcely terrify her.

Two months had passed since Millicent's examination before Mr. Justice Bowers, and nothing had been seen of Darrell Markham. Brief letters came now and then for Sarah Pecker, telling her how the young man was hard at work for the good of his cousin; but each of these letters was less hopeful than the last, and Sarah began to despair of any help from that quarter for the hapless prisoner languishing in Carlisle jail.

Sarah had traveled to see her old master's daughter, and each time had found Mrs. Duke equally calm and resigned; pale, and thin, and faded, it is true, but less altered than Sally thought to find her by this long imprisonment.

Once, and once only, Millicent uttered some words that struck a shivering horror to the very heart of the listener.

It was towards the close of her dreary incarceration that Mrs. Duke thus terrified her honest-hearted friend. Sarah had been reading Darrell's last letter, in which, though evidently wrestling very hard with despair, he promised that he would labor to the very death to clear his cousin's name, when Millicent began wringing her hands and crying mournfully:—'Why does Darrell take this trouble for me? Let the worst that can befall me, I have little wish to live; and after all, Sarah—after all, who can tell that I am really guiltless of George Duke's blood?'

'Miss Millicent!—Miss Millicent!'

'Who can tell? I know that I was nigh upon being distraught that cruel night upon which my husband came home. Who knows if it may not be as Mr. Bowers thinks, that I killed him in a paroxysm of madness? Heaven knows that I was close enough to madness that night.'

'Oh, Miss Milly!' she cried, 'for pity's sake—for the sake of the merciful God who looks down upon you and sees your helplessness, do not utter these horrible words. Do you know that to say in the court of justice one week hence what you have said to me this day, would be to doom yourself to certain death. *I* know, Miss Millicent, that you are innocent, and *you* know it too. Never, never, never let that thought leave your brain; for when it does, you will be mad! Remember, whatever others may think of you—however the wisest in the land may judge you;—remember through all, and until death—if death must come—that you are innocent!'

Sarah Pecker did not content herself with this adjuration, she waited upon the governor of the jail, and being admitted to his presence, implored of him that he would place some kind and discreet woman in the cell with Mrs. Duke, as nurse, or watcher, for that the poor lady was in danger of losing her wits from the effects of long and solitary confinement. 'I would ask leave to stay with her myself, poor darling,' Sarah said, 'but that I have one lying ill at home whose days are well nigh numbered.'

Mrs. Pecker spoke with a heartfelt energy that carried conviction with it; and although those were no great days for mercy, and though the glorious fiction of the law which pretends to hold a man innocent until the hour of his condemnation was then little attended to, the governor acceded to Sarah's prayer, and a woman (herself doing penance for some petty offence) was placed with Millicent to lighten the horrors of her cell.

Sarah had her hands full of trouble this melancholy spring She had told so much of her son's story as she well dared to Samuel Pecker; telling him, however, that the pedlar was the brother of her dead husband, Thomas Masterson, and telling very little of her son's delinquencies. She also told him that which is apt to soften the sternest of us towards the sinning; she told him that whatever Henry Masterson's failings might have been, he would soon be beyond the chance of making any earthly atonement for them, and before a Judge who was wiser, yet more pitiful than any Justice in the county of Cumberland, or on the face of the wide earth.

So simple and soft-hearted Samuel Pecker opened his arms to the dying son of the vagabond Thomas Masterson; and the worthy Thomas, after having enjoyed a good night's rest and a hearty breakfast, strode away in the dusky dawn of the February day; after leaving behind him a message for Mrs. Pecker, to the effect that he should return before the week was out to fetch that little matter they had talked about.

Betty delivered this message with laudable accuracy, and Mrs. Pecker fully understood that the little matter in question was the hundred pounds she had promised as the price of the pedlar's secret. She obtained the sum with little difficulty from her confiding husband, who went by coach to the market-town one afternoon within the week, to draw the money from the bank; but it happened that on that very afternoon Thomas Masterson, dressed in a new suit bought by him out of a handful of ready cash obtained from Sarah on the night of their interview, swaggered through the high street of the same market-town, and was betrayed into the natural weakness of putting his big hand into somebody else's pocket. Whether from long residence in a foreign land, and want of practice in the art, I know not, but Thomas on that particular afternoon was so very far from up to the mark in his performance, that he was caught in the act by his intended victim, and delivered over to the constables, who handed him on to Carlise jail to await his trial at the ensuing assizes, with many others of the same calibre.

This unfortunate circumstance of course prevented his appearing to claim the reward promised by Sarah, and the worthy woman, after living for several days and nights in perpetual dread of his arrival, began to hope that some happy chance had befallen to send him out of her way.

She had enough to do in watching by the sick-bed of her son, who lay in a comfortable garret chamber under the roof of the house, and whose whereabouts were known to none but his mother, Samuel Pecker, and the doctor who attended upon him.

The brilliant Sir Lovel Mortimer—the notorious Captain Fanny—could scarcely have had a safer hiding-place than the garret chamber in this old inn. Bow-street had grown weary of counting on the reward that was freely offered for his capture. His old comrades—fine fellows, of course, every one of them, but any one of whom might have taken it into his head to turn king's evidence at a push —had entirely lost sight of him; and it seemed almost as if the highwayman had dropped out of the troubled sea of human life and crime, without leaving so much as a bubble to mark the spot where he had gone down.

CHAPTER XXIV.—THE TRIAL OF MILLICENT DUKE.

Darrell Markham had not been idle. The noble Scottish gentleman whom he served was ready to give him all help in his hour of need, and three days after the examination before Mr. Montague Bowers, the case of Millicent Duke was in the hands of the most distinguished criminal lawyers of the day. Busy Bow-street runners—better known as Robin-redbreasts—had been placed upon the scent; but look which way they would at the case, it had an equally sinister aspect, and Darrell Markham's hardest trial was to find that even those who were most friendly to him had no belief in the innocence of his wretched cousin.

'That the unhappy lady committed this terrible deed in a paroxysm of madness, and that she is morally innocent of the crime of murder, I can easily believe, my dear Darrell,' said Lord C——; 'but that any English jury will acquit her upon the evidence of which you tell me is more than I dare to hope.'

Endeavours to throw light upon the antecedents of George Duke resulted in the discovery that the Captain of the *Vulture* had well deserved the worst fate that could befall him. Inquiries which occupied much time, and caused a great deal of trouble in the making, revealed the fact that the good ship *Vulture* had been seized and burnt by a vessel belonging to the French Government off the coast of Barbary; and that, her captain, George Duke, together with his first mate, one Thomas Masterson, had been sent to the galleys by the same French Government as slavers, pirates, and suspected assassins; from which fate they had escaped in conjunction, upon the first of January in that year.

Yes, George Duke, the dashing sailor, who had so easily imposed upon ignorant Squire Markham with his naval uniform and flashy manners, had been a rogue and a pirate, and had worked at the oar with his ex-mate Thomas Masterson for upwards of six years.

The attorney employed by Darrell Markham for the preparation of his cousin's defence, deemed it expedient to discover the whereabouts of this very Thomas Masterson, in the hope that some clue to the mystery might be extracted from this the familiar companion of the murdered man.

An advertisement inserted several times in the *London Gazette*, resulted in a letter from the governor of Carlisle jail, containing the information that this man, Thomas Masterson, was confined in that prison for some petty theft, awaiting his trial at the same assizes which were to decide the fate of Mrs. George Duke.

One of the best men at the Old Bailey was retained for Millicent's defence by the solicitors entrusted with the case. Darrell Markham implored the worthy gentleman to spare neither trouble nor money in compassing the acquittal of his unhappy cousin; but the advocate shook his head over the contents of his brief, and freely told Mr. Markham that he did not see a glimmer of hope in the dreary business.

So, on the eve of Millicent's trial, the northern mail carried Darrell Markham, Mr. Pauncet, the solicitor, and Mr. Horace Weldon, barrister-at-law, to the city of Carlisle, where, upon the terrible morrow, a delicate woman of seven-and-twenty years of age was to answer to the charge of willful murder.

The eve of the trial brought Sarah Pecker from the bedside of her dying son. The poor woman came to Carlisle attended by Samuel, who was one of the witnesses for the Crown, and whose brain was well nigh turned by the responsibilities of his position.

The cold march sunshine lighted up every corner of the crowded court when Millicent Duke was led to her place in the criminal dock to answer to the charge of murder. She was brought so low in health by her long imprisonment, that her custodians, out of pity for her weak state, allowed her to sit throughout the proceedings.

Fifty years after that day there were people living in Carlisle who could tell of the pale golden head, lighted by the faint spring sunshine, and the delicate face, worn and wasted by trial and suffering, but very beautiful in its white tranquility.

'Not guilty.'

The evidence given by the witnesses for the prosecution was much the same as that already cited before Mr. Montague Bowers. Again Samuel Pecker became vague and obscure as to the identity of George Duke, of the *Vulture*, with that ghost, or shadow, which had appeared at three divers times to three separate individuals in the course of seven years.